Sam grabbed warm, masculine fingers. AJ's.

Electricity, so strong she wondered if the outlet were live, shot up her arm. She closed her eyes against the yearning building deep inside her. It swelled and threatened to erupt. She couldn't let anything happen. She had to be strong. Fight it. She had to—

Then she felt his arm drawing small, slow circles on the back of her hand. The electricity returned, shooting to all endpoints of her body, bringing them to life in a way she had never experienced. She tried to pull away, but he tightened his hold.

In a last-ditch effort to stop what seemed inevitable, Sam made a feeble attempt to force him to halt. "AJ. Don't…"

"Why, Sam? We both want it." His breath feathered her face, warm and sweet. His mouth… Lord help her, his mouth. It was close, so very close. So tempting, so—

She closed her eyes.

Dear Reader,

When I tried to find a reason why I chose to write this book, all I could come up with initially was that it's the sequel to *Baptism in Fire*. However, as I wrote the book and it took on a life of its own, as it always does, my purpose became clearer. A long time ago, a dear friend told me that I wrote healing books. This one turned out to be no different.

Aside from the fact that, as always, my characters became a part of my life, the book became an account of how much we miss out on by not allowing people we feel have wronged us to explain themselves. Things are too often not what they appear to be on the surface.

No, I'm not going to preach. You'll have to read this book to discover what I mean. I am just going to ask you to be tolerant of other people. Something my mother used to say comes to mind—*Don't judge a book by its cover.* Look beneath the surface. You'll be surprised by what you may find lurking there.

Happy reading.

Blessings!

Elizabeth Sinclair

Elizabeth Sinclair

TOUCHED BY FIRE

Silhouette®

Romantic

SUSPENSE

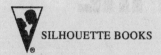

SILHOUETTE BOOKS

ISBN-13: 978-0-373-27556-4
ISBN-10: 0-373-27556-0

TOUCHED BY FIRE

Visit Silhouette Books at www.eHarlequin.com

Printed in U.S.A.

Books by Elizabeth Sinclair

Silhouette Romantic Suspense

Jenny's Castle #606
Baptism in Fire #1429
Touched by Fire #1486

ELIZABETH SINCLAIR

In 1988 Elizabeth's husband, Bob, dragged her kicking and screaming from her birthplace, the scenic Hudson Valley of Upstate New York, to historic St. Augustine, Florida. It took her about three seconds to stop struggling and to fall deeply in love with her adopted hometown. Shortly after their move, at 3:47 p.m. on August 3, 1992, she sold her first romance novel, *Jenny's Castle*.

Despite the fact that Elizabeth used to spend hours in the kitchen cooking big meals, Bob, her most ardent supporter, has learned to enjoy hot dogs and delivery pizza as much as he used to enjoy spaghetti sauce from scratch. Oh, and he no longer complains about all the books she spends money on. Bob and Elizabeth have three children, four lovely grandchildren, a rambunctious sheltie, Ripley, and an affectionate adopted beagle, Sammi Girl, which they found abandoned along the roadside and took into their home.

Elizabeth is the author of several books for Silhouette Romantic Suspense and Harlequin American Romance. For more about Elizabeth, visit her Web site at www.elizabethsinclair.com.

Dedication:

To Leslie King for the strength, love and support
she's given her mom, my dear friend, at a time
when she needed it most.

Acknowledgments:

A big Thank You to the guys in the
Electronics Department at the St. Augustine, Florida,
Home Depot, who left their supper uneaten to give this
electronically challenged writer a lesson in how a remote
control could work a tape recorder. Thanks, gentlemen.

Chapter 1

His hands moved expertly over her hot flesh, bringing it to life, bringing her to life in a way that made her squirm beneath him. What was he waiting for? Why didn't he give her what she wanted, what she ached for?

"Please," she pleaded, her nails digging into his shoulders.

"Not yet," he growled against her swollen breast. "First, tell me you love me, that you trust me."

He circled the aching tip of her breast with his tongue, sending wave after wave of intense longing through her. The teasing was excruciating. Her body throbbed with need.

She couldn't stand any more of this torture. She had to say it. She had to—or die from the gnawing need inside her. She opened her mouth to speak the words that would release her from this sensual prison, but they wouldn't come. Every time she tried to tell him she trusted him, loved him, she felt as though a large hole had opened beneath her, a hole that would swallow her up the moment the words passed her lips, a hole from which she would never escape and the fall would be more painful than she could stand.

"Say them, Sam. Say the words."

"I can't," she sobbed. "I just…can't."

"Then there will be no release for you." He rolled off her, leaving her emotionally hungry and physically cold.

"No!" she cried. "No!" She reached for him, but she found only air.

Her eyes flew open.

She bolted upright and looked at the empty bed beside her. Slowly the haze of sleep receded, and she realized it had all been a dream. The fabric of her nightgown stuck to her sweat-slicked body. Her hair hung in tangles around her tear-dampened face. The night air sent chills over her, despite the fact that her body was so hot, she could almost smell the smoke coming from it.

Pushing her hair from her eyes, she buried her hot face in her hands. "Samantha Ellis, you're committing emotional suicide, and it has to stop. Now!"

Sam didn't make a habit of talking to herself, but mental admonitions didn't seem to be working anymore. If she didn't get a handle on this crazy obsession with Chief of Detectives A. J. Branson, she'd be serving up her heart to him on a silver platter, and he'd slice it to ribbons.

Sam had already been through that pain with Sloan

Whitley, the onetime love of her life, when he neglected to tell her he was married; she was not about to do it again. When she'd added Sloan to the lineup of betrayals by her family, her quota had been filled to overflowing. After the Sloan fiasco, she'd locked her heart away and sworn there would be no more relationships, and certainly not with A.J., a man with a trail of heartbreaks and a history of running from commitment. But if she didn't get control of this attraction she was nursing for the handsome blond detective, she might well find herself back in her old room at the Heartbreak Hotel.

Disgusted with her frustrating lack of ability to control her feelings, Sam rolled over in bed and glanced at the bedside clock's illuminated dial. 5:33 a.m. The alarm would sound in another hour, and she didn't see herself falling back to sleep. Might as well call it a night. Free of the disturbing, erotic dreams of the Orange Grove, Florida detective, dreams that had become all too common of late and all too disturbing, she sat up, hit the off button and rubbed her eyes.

Determined not to give A.J. any more of her time, she threw back the damp sheets, slid from the bed, grabbed her robe and then headed to the kitchen to put on a pot of wake-up coffee. As she passed through the hall and into the living room, she rubbed at her throbbing temples. Lack of sleep had brought on a headache that was quickly increasing in strength to the point that it felt as if someone was twisting an ax in her skull.

She'd taken two steps into the living room when she detected an odor she and every other firefighter knew well. Smoke. A remnant of her all-too-vivid dream? But she was wide-awake now. She sniffed the air again.

Burning fabric.

Instantly alert, headache forgotten, her firefighter training kicked in. She ran through the house searching for the source. It didn't take long to find it. Just a few feet from the front door, thick gray curls of smoke poured from under an armchair and had begun to accumulate in a misty layer along the ceiling.

"What the..."

Despite her bordering-on-petite size, she upended the heavy chair and found a plain white, smoldering, business-size envelope beneath it. Automatically, she scooped it up by a corner. Racing to the front door and nearly falling on the highly polished cypress floor, she unlocked the door and yanked it open, then ran to the edge of the porch and threw the envelope onto the dew-wet grass.

With the emergency in the past, the surge of adrenaline that had driven her dissipated—just as it always did after every fire she'd ever attended—leaving her drained and emotionally exhausted.

Then realization of what had just happened and its possible outcome hit her between the eyes.

I could have died. And my home could have burned to the ground.

For anyone else the specter of possible death would have been trauma enough, but for Sam, who had spent her entire childhood hopping from motel room to motel room, the destruction of her home almost outweighed her own mortality. To lose her house would be like losing herself and everything she'd worked for since she'd separated herself from the nomadic life her mother had forced on her and her sister for years. This house wasn't just a brick-and-mortar structure. It was *home*, the very foundation of her independence, her symbol of security and stability. Aftershock set in.

Her hands began to shake, and her knees threatened to fold like an accordion beneath her. She collapsed against the porch railing. Her heart pounded in her ears. Sweat beaded her forehead and coated the palms of her trembling hands. Her empty stomach churned with sour fear.

Taking a deep breath to calm herself, she stared at the smoking envelope. A part-time arson investigator, she didn't have to wonder what had caused the envelope to smolder. She'd learned about them in her basic training at the firefighters' academy, and she'd seen them in the line of duty. As a result, she knew all too well what had caused the spontaneous combustion— hand lotion and potassium permanganate, or some variety thereof.

It was a simple, cheap, insidious device that initially just produced a lot of smoke, but if left to reach its full potential, could cause untold damage. She busied her mind by repeating by rote the steps of its creation.

Hand lotion went into the bottom of the envelope, then it was folded. The potassium was added and the envelope folded again. When the fire-starter got to the scene, he had only to unfold the envelope, shake it to mix the two ingredients together, place it somewhere where it wouldn't be quickly discovered and walk casually away. The ingredients would first begin to smoke, then eventually erupt into open flame. Ideally, no one would know it was there until it was too late. The fire would start long after the arsonist had left the scene undetected, and any evidence would almost certainly be consumed by the fire. Rudimentary, but deadly.

The torch—or arsonist—had taken a calculated risk that Sam wouldn't find it in time to put it out. He had probably counted on her sleeping through the preliminary stages and waking when the fire had already taken hold—hopefully, when it was out of control.

But how did he get it in the house? Everything had been locked up tight. Sam lived alone, and she was smart enough not to take chances with security. This house represented the first real home she'd ever known, and she had guarded against it being invaded in any way. That it had been gave rise to a mixture of fear, indignation and anger.

She glanced toward the open door and at once knew how this had happened. The torch hadn't gotten inside. He'd shoved it through the mail slot in the door. But because of her highly polished floors, when it hit the slick wood, it had probably slid forward, stopping only because it had come in contact with the dust ruffle of the overstuffed chair, accidentally making it more deadly and efficient than the arsonist intended.

Now that she had figured out how it got there, two even more disturbing questions drummed at her mind:

Who had planted the device?

Why would anyone want to burn down her house and possibly her with it?

Though she racked her brain, no one came to mind. Sam was a very private person with only a few friends. To her knowledge, she had no enemies. But since she and Rachel Sutherland had formed FIST, the Fire Investigation Special Team, she had nailed a few property owners who had torched their buildings for the insurance money. Could it be one of them? That was the only thing that came close to making any sense. But if so, which one was ticked off enough at her to want her dead?

While she'd been trying to sort through who could have done this, the wetness from the dew-laden grass had seeped into the paper and the envelope had stopped smoldering. Now that it no longer presented a threat, she picked it up by one corner and carried it back inside, slipped it into a brown craft envelope and sealed it, then marked it with her name, the time and date, and the words *incendiary device,* then put it beside her purse.

For a moment, she considered giving it to A.J., but that would mean seeing him, and she knew all too well what happened each time she saw him. She turned into an emotional heap who could think of little beyond how much she wanted to give in to her desires. Maybe Rachel's detective husband, Luke Sutherland, could pass it on to his boss.

But first things first. She went to the garage, removed a piece of wood from an old packing crate she'd hung on to, found some nails and a hammer and nailed the wood over the mail slot. That would do until she could have the door replaced with a slotless one. Back in the living room, she threw open the phone book and searched the yellow pages for the name of a carpenter. While she did so, she continued to try to make sense of all this, always returning to the same question.

Who wanted to kill her?

Deep in thought, A. J. Branson stared down at the official-looking letter in his hand. He hadn't expected such a quick reply to his application. At least he'd been given a few months' time to make a decision. Frowning, he rubbed absently at his forehead. Outside his office door the noise of the squad room drifted to him as Orange Grove's finest arrived for night duty. Automatically, his free hand reached for a cigar that would have, until he'd given them up months ago, resided in a humidor on his cluttered desk.

"Don't tell me. The president has asked you to come up with a solution for world peace."

Starting guiltily, A.J. withdrew his hand, then looked up to find Luke Sutherland, one of his detectives and his best friend, standing in the doorway, a brown craft envelope in his hand.

A.J. chuckled, but the sound held no humor. "Nothing that earth-shattering, I'm afraid."

"Oh? Sure looked serious to me. What else would make you reach for a cigar that hasn't been there since last year?" Luke grinned and dropped into the chair facing A.J., then steepled his fingers beneath his chin and studied his boss. "Want to talk about it?"

Did he? A.J. wasn't sure he was ready to share this with anyone. But this was his friend. He'd been the best man at Luke's wedding. Together they'd lived through Luke's child being kidnapped and thought dead, his breakup with Rachel, a series of fires that had threatened Rachel's life and the final capture of the arsonist/kidnapper and rescue of little Maggie and her mother. The reunited Sutherlands had even named their son after him and made him Jay's godfather. If he could share this with anyone, Luke would be that person.

"It's a job offer from the New York State Bureau of Criminal Investigation."

"The BCI?" Luke sat up straight, alarm written all over his features. "You're leaving Orange Grove? What the hell for?"

"It means a promotion and a big pay raise."

Luke shook his head. "You could apply to the Florida Department of Law Enforcement. If NY wants you, Florida should, too. Dammit, A.J. This is going to sound selfish as hell, but why would you go to NY?"

First and foremost, the simple answer was that this job had been something he'd wanted for a long time, something he'd set as a goal for himself long ago. When a friend had alerted him to the possibility of an opening months ago, he'd jumped at it with nothing more than his career in mind. Now, however, he had another reason.

The other reason was *not* something A.J. was ready to share with anyone, even Luke. How could he tell him that this job offer gave him the perfect excuse to get away from Samantha Ellis? Or that he was running away from his heart because he was becoming more and more attracted to Sam with each passing day, and it scared him senseless? He was, after all, a cop, the chief of detectives, for heaven's sake. How could one woman make him want to run fifteen hundred miles away for emotional cover?

It didn't take much effort to find the answer: one failed marriage, followed by a failed engagement. When it came to women, he was batting zero in the relationship department and had learned not to trust his choices. Sam could just be another emotional disaster waiting to happen, and he could not take that risk. A heart could take just so much abuse, and commitment seemed to be his own personal battering ram.

"Damn! You're going, aren't you?" Luke asked, a thread of shock imbuing his voice.

A.J. shrugged. "I haven't made any decisions." But, truth be told, he was *seriously* considering it, and he'd been given some time to make up his mind. "I have to think it through."

"What's to think about?" Luke asked, standing and beginning to pace A.J.'s small office. "Good grief, A.J., all your friends are here. You have a good job. What the hell more could you want?"

A family. Kids. Love. Everything you have. Some kind of guarantee that Sam won't be just another mistake to add to my list of personal screwups.

But he didn't voice his thoughts. He didn't need Luke lecturing him about his track record with women. He could run his personal life without any help from Luke.

And you've done such a splendid job so far.

A.J.'s nerves were drawn as tight as a bowstring.

He'd had enough of Luke nudging him and reminding him of what he'd be leaving or what he'd never have. "Don't you have work to do?" he asked, putting on his *boss* face and effectively closing the discussion.

Luke threw him an impatient look, then tossed the brown envelope he'd been holding facedown on A.J.'s desk. "You should see this." Then he left the office, closing the door with more gusto than was needed.

A.J. shoved the envelope aside and leaned back in his chair, closed his eyes and sighed. When had his life gotten so complicated? He laughed aloud. The day he'd met Samantha Ellis outside the arson task force room. That's when.

He could still see the blue highlights in her silky, raven-black hair shining in the sunlight and her sea-blue eyes twinkling up at him. He could still feel the tightening in his gut that always signaled the beginning of an attraction to a woman. He could still feel the wash of warmth that went over him when she'd smiled. If he'd been smart, he would have backed away then, distanced himself, but he hadn't and now he was paying the price.

Most disconcerting of all was that when he was around her all his good intentions, all his firm resolutions to keep his distance, melted away like snow under a noonday sun. In his heart, he knew he was getting down to the wire. If he didn't put distance between them soon, they'd both suffer the consequences. The offer he'd so coveted from the BCI just provided the escape route.

Heaving a sigh, he sat up, turned over the envelope Luke had given him, then—after reading Sam's name scrawled across the front—tore it open. Carefully, he slid the scorched contents onto his desk. For a time he stared at it, unable to distinguish what it was, then it came to him. Sam gave this to Rachel? Why? He glanced at the front of the envelope again and read Sam's address on it and the words *incendiary device*. His heart felt as if someone had reached into his chest and squeezed it as hard as they could. Then his anger began to bubble to the surface. What the hell was this all about?

He strode to his door, threw it open and bellowed for Luke to come back to his office.

Late the next day, when they'd returned from a small, drought-induced brush fire, the third one that day, Sam checked the pressure in her SCBA. She hadn't had to use her self-contained breathing apparatus this time but, out of habit, she checked the pressure before stowing it away. Satisfied that everything was acceptable, she placed it back on the fire truck's side rack, then turned her attention to her new partner, Kevin Hilary, a young rookie fresh out of the academy. He'd only been with the company for a few weeks, and Chief Santelli had asked her to keep an eye on him and teach him all she could. It was the first time in her life that someone had looked to her for knowledge, and not a means to an end, so she took the job very seriously.

She smiled at what appeared to be brown oil stains dotting Kevin's hands and pants. Having met Kevin's mother on several occasions, Sam knew for sure that when the domineering woman saw the stained pants, she'd probably chew him a new derriere. Poor kid. Sam wasn't sure who had it worse: her with a mother that had only cared about the money she brought in winning children's beauty pageants, or Kevin with a mother that oversaw every aspect of his life and dictated how he should lead it.

She laughed to herself. If his disheveled hair meant anything, Kevin was into getting his job done with dedication. One thing his mother hadn't seemed to have dampened was Kevin's eagerness to excel at his job.

A frown pleated her brow. There had been a time when that same eagerness had resided inside her, too, but lately, though she still loved her job, she'd detected a distinct waning of that zest she'd always felt for being a firefighter.

Taking a deep, cleansing breath, she leaned over Kevin. "How you doing, probie?"

Kevin looked up, his face screwed up in a serious expression. "I'm finished with the SCBA check. The other equipment is done, too."

"Okay. Put it back in the rack. We need to get to the kitchen. It's our turn to make supper and those vultures will be screaming like banshees if they don't get fed."

Their twenty-four-hour shift had ended an hour earlier, so Sam sent Kevin home. Before she left, she'd double-checked his equipment to make sure he hadn't overlooked anything. Finding everything in order, Sam gathered her purse and turned to leave the firehouse. Her heart skidded into her throat. The one man on this planet she didn't want to see was walking toward her.

A. J. Branson's blond hair shone golden in the sunlight pouring through the open apparatus bay doors. The muscles in his thighs and arms rippled beneath his white shirt and navy slacks. His burgundy tie had been pulled to half-mast. Two open buttons on his white shirt revealed his tanned throat and the very top of his bare chest.

Sam caught her breath and tried to arrange her features in an expression that didn't give away her sudden urge to jump his bones on the oil-stained floor.

Not until he was almost in front of her did she notice what he was carrying—the brown craft envelope containing the incendiary device she'd found under the chair and had dropped off at Rachel's. Dammit! She knew, because A.J. headed up the arson task force, that Luke would eventually give it to A.J. and that he would come to her for details. She hadn't expected him to be this mad.

A.J.'s tight expression sent a chill of dread racing over her. He was really upset that she hadn't come directly to him. Company protocol dictated that the envelope should have gone to him and not a detective. As a firefighter and member of FIST, she knew that. She'd just been trying to get around what evidently was about to happen anyway: a face-to-face confrontation with the one man in Orange Grove who could raise her blood pressure several notches.

A.J. stopped directly in front of her, his broad shoulders blocking out almost everything else in the room. The smell of his aftershave mixed with the smell of diesel fuel and oil, but her well-trained, discerning nose singled out his particular scent and sent a frantic message directly to her nerve endings. Her talent for being able to detect certain accelerants simply by smell had always been a distinct benefit to her as a firefighter and now at FIST, but right now it was a definite drawback.

Her control over her rebellious senses spun off into the ether like the head of a dandelion in a brisk wind.

A.J. held out the envelope and glared at her. When he finally spoke, the sharp edges of his tone were tightly controlled and teetering on the fringe of suppressed anger. "Care to explain what this means and why it came to my attention by way of Luke Sutherland?"

Chapter 2

Sam stalled for time. She looked past A.J.'s glowering frown to the streak of Florida sunlight bathing the floor in front of the open apparatus bay doors. Though the sun had started its descent, heat waves still rose from the pavement outside, attesting to the temperature having hit the mid-nineties that day. Because the heat still lingered, the early evening activity on the street consisted of just a young boy riding his bicycle, a woman pushing a baby stroller and an older man headed in the direction of the bench situated in the shade of a large oak tree right across the street from the firehouse.

"Well?" A.J. said, yanking Sam from the distractions. He brandished the envelope. "When did you plan on letting me know that someone tried to burn your house down?"

She shrugged, now feeling very foolish about bypassing A.J. Was she that apprehensive about being in a room with the man for a few minutes? Did she have that little control over herself? This was getting totally out of hand. She couldn't arrange her life around A. J. Branson.

"I figured Luke would tell you." She ventured an innocent smile, hoping her explanation would be adequate, and that it would cool his anger and clear the tension draining her nerves. But his frown only deepened.

A.J. stiffened and, rather than abating under her smile, his anger seemed to intensify.

"I don't give a flying fig who got the information first. What I care about is what could have happened to you."

Sam blinked. Her heart lurched. Had she heard that right? Did A.J. really care about what happened to her? Don't read anything into that, she told herself. He'd care about anyone. That it was you means nothing special. She opened her mouth to make a retort, but before she could, Chief Joe Santelli joined them.

"Should I get out the gloves? You two look like you're ready to go a couple of rounds right here."

Damn! She didn't want her boss to know about this. He'd just make a big deal about nothing. And it *was* nothing, she told herself for the umpteenth time that day. If she let it become something, then she'd have to admit that she was scared spineless, and she wouldn't do that. She would not give whomever planted the incendiary device that much power.

"A.J.'s just blowing this whole thing way out of proportion." Before A.J. could retort, she picked up her purse, slung it over her shoulder and then elbowed her way past the two men. "Now, if you'll excuse me, I have a date with a hot bubble bath."

"Out of proportion?" A.J. roared behind her.

Sam closed her ears to him and kept moving. As she walked away from them, she pushed the button on her car remote earlier than usual. It would start her car and get the AC busy cooling off the interior so she wouldn't have to climb into the stifling heat of the closed SUV.

Instantly, an ear-splitting explosion shook the firehouse.

The whole scene took on a surreal quality. Firefighters carrying fire extinguishers rushed past her. The old man on the park bench bolted to his feet, his mouth forming an O like those plastic Christmas carolers Sam put on her coffee table every year. Directly in front of her, on the edge of the parking lot, a huge fireball burned, the flames leaping wildly toward the darkening sky. In the center of the fire was her SUV. She watched in stunned silence as the firefighters sprayed it with foam from the extinguishers.

Then it hit her. When the car exploded, she could have been in it. *You* should *have been in it,* an insidious voice whispered.

She should have died, just like she should have died when she found the incendiary device. A cold sweat broke out on her forehead. Her hands began to tremble uncontrollably. Her stomach heaved, and her knees began to cave.

Strong arms enveloped her and guided her back into

the firehouse to Joe Santelli's office. When she looked up, she saw A.J.'s concerned face looking down at her.

His legs no more adequate to support him than Sam's seemed to be, A.J. pulled a chair up and sat facing her, their knees inches apart. "You okay?" His voice shook as badly as his insides. What if Sam had been in her car?

"I'm…not…sure," she said, her voice shaky, her face a ghostly white. "It's not every day…you get to see…your car…blown up, is it?" She tried to smile, but the corners of her mouth trembled and ruined the effect.

A.J. took her shaking hand firmly in his. He wanted so much to take her in his arms and make sure she was safe, but in his gut he knew that would be a temporary safety. No one had to tell him that this jerk would try again and again—and wouldn't stop until he was caught or Sam was dead.

Just thinking about such a thing made A.J. wince with pain, as if someone had reached into his chest and pulled out his heart. He tightened his grip on her hand until she cried out and pulled it out of his grasp. He looked at her.

From the return of color to her face and the tight set of her mouth, it seemed that the pain had roused Sam from the shock. The old in-your-face Sam had emerged ready to do battle. She opened her mouth but before she could speak Chief Santelli entered the office shaking his head.

His pale face and awed expression told A.J. that the violent destruction of Sam's car had shaken him, too. "They got the fire out. Now, does someone want to help me make some sense of what just happened out there? In short, what the hell's going on?"

"Maybe this will help," A.J. said, and turned out the contents of the brown envelope onto Santelli's desktop. "Sam found this in her house yesterday morning." Sam glared at him, but he ignored her.

A.J. stared down at the items spread out before him: a partially burned, white business envelope; a few small purple crystals of potassium permanganate that hadn't gotten a chance to dissolve, thanks to Sam's quick thinking; and a few drops of opaque hand lotion that hadn't been totally consumed. A mixture that, if left to do its intended job, would have set Sam's house on fire while she slept. Just the thought made A.J.'s stomach sour.

Santelli looked at the debris on the desk, swore softly, glanced at the firemen milling around the apparatus bay and then frowned at Sam. "I'll be right back. We need to talk." He got up and left the office.

"Thanks a lot," Sam snapped. She rose and began pacing the office.

"Sam, I—"

"Don't," she said, holding up her hand. "I have to think."

A.J. concentrated on returning the pieces of the incendiary device to the envelope, but, though he tried his best not to watch, he couldn't ignore the seductive sway of her hips as she walked. His traitorous mind flew to imagining her in a dress, black and slinky. One cut down to the equator in the front and backless. One that would expose her tanned skin to his view. One that would sway against her long legs and mold to her hips and thighs. One that—

"Ellis?"

A.J. started. Blinking, he looked up to find Santelli had come back.

"Park it." He pointed to the chair beside A.J. Sam resumed her seat wordlessly.

Santelli leaned back in the squeaky desk chair. "Okay, Sam, do you want to tell me what this is all about?"

Sam briefly recounted the events of the previous morning, leading up to and ending with her finding the incendiary device. As she spoke, A.J. quietly fumed at the idea of someone invading Sam's house and endangering her life. But he managed to hold his tongue.

When she'd finished, Santelli leaned his forearms on his desk. "Any idea who would do any of this?"

Sam shook her head. "None. I've racked my brain, and I can't come up with anyone except maybe an irate property owner who got miffed because I proved his fire was intentionally set. But even then, I don't recall any of them being especially ticked off at me for ruining their claim." She took a deep breath and waited while Santelli digested all she'd said.

A.J. studied the relatively new chief of Engine Company 108. Joe Santelli, a middle-aged man who had risen quickly through the ranks and been promoted to chief of the company a few months previous, had a reputation as a no-nonsense type of guy. A.J. suppressed a smile. Knowing that Sam was as headstrong as they came, he could imagine how this cramped her gung-ho style, not to mention made Santelli's life… interesting, to say the least.

It was common knowledge that Santelli had an almost obsessive need to keep his firefighters safe. A.J. was more than certain that Santelli would take radical steps to see to Sam's safety. He was equally as sure that Sam would rebel against anything that kept her from doing her job, despite the risk.

"I don't like this, Ellis," Santelli finally said, then turned to A.J. "You're going to check the envelope for prints, right?"

A.J. nodded.

"The police are checking over the car for anything they can find, which probably won't be much. Since your car was toward the back of the lot, it's pretty safe to say that no one saw the bomb being installed." Santelli sighed heavily, then turned back to Sam. "Until we get some results from the crime lab, Ellis, I'm taking you off the truck and putting you on the duty desk."

A.J. cringed and glanced at Sam for her reaction.

Sam's entire body went into resistance mode. "What?" She shot out of the chair, her voice raised and demanding. Santelli threw her a quelling look, and she slumped back in her seat and adopted a more respectful, but no less urgent, tone. "Why?"

"Any whack-job who had enough guts to shove this thing in your mail slot with the intent of burning you up—and then blow up your car in the fire department parking lot—is not going to like it that his schemes failed," Santelli explained patiently.

"But—"

"Santelli's right, Sam. This jerk is going to keep trying," A.J. offered.

Sam sent him a scathing glare as if to say Santelli didn't need any help from him, the chief was wrecking her life quite well on his own. A.J., on the other hand, was using his own unique wrecking ball, and it had nothing to do with envelopes and fire—at least not the kind of fire set with matches.

"Do you think I don't know that he'll try again?" she snapped. "Taking me off the truck isn't going to change that. Besides, if I'm on the truck, I'd have all the guys around for protection."

"And you really believe that will stop this nutcase?" Santelli countered, his expression telling them he didn't believe it, and he doubted that Sam really did, either.

Sam seemed to wilt like a flower lacking water. Though relieved that she'd be removed from danger, A.J. felt for her. Any fool could see that firefighting was her life. To take that from her was like depriving her of air.

"Okay, I'll concede that he may try again, but I still don't see why you have to take me off the truck." Sam's deflated voice tore at A.J.'s heart.

Despite his agreement with Santelli's decision and how much it eased his own anxiety, A.J. knew these were going to be the longest few days of Sam's life. He made a mental note to hurry things up in the lab as much as he could to get Sam back on her beloved fire truck.

"Aside from the fact that you'll be a sitting duck riding on top of that truck and exposed to any nut job at the fire scenes," Santelli went on, "fires are danger-ous enough. I need my attention on *all* my firefighters, not on who's trying to do one of them in. And they need their attention on the fire, not on playing bodyguard for you. I want you here, where I can be sure of what's going on." When she opened her mouth to resume her protest, he raised a hand. "End of discussion, Ellis."

Saying nothing, Sam glared at the chief, revolt written all over her features.

Santelli remained silent for a moment, then smiled. "There *is* another way, Ellis."

She brightened. "What?"

"I can suspend you from duty and send you home until the police solve this."

"But that could take—"

"Months," A.J. interjected. When he saw her expression crumple, he tried to soften the blow. "Of course, you never know. It could be solved as soon as the fingerprints come back. I'll make sure they get top priority, Sam." Seeing the defeated sag of her shoulders, A.J. felt Sam had suffered enough trauma for one day. He stood. "If you're through, Santelli, I'll take Sam home."

"Yes, I'm through."

Sam stood and fixed A.J. with cold blue eyes. "No thanks. You've already done quite enough. I'll get one of the guys to drive me."

"I said *I'll* take you home," A.J. said, his tone brooking no argument. If he had his way, he'd never let her out of his sight, but he knew she'd never agree to that in a million years. "Until this is solved, I don't want you going anywhere alone, and I want you to lock your doors when you're at home."

She glared at A.J., then Santelli. The chief gave a nod of agreement. "Fine. I'll wait in the dining room." Then she stalked out.

A.J. walked to the door. Through the window he watched Sam storm across the apparatus bay toward the stairs that lead to the upper floor, where the dining room and kitchen were located, hating himself for his part in this. Dust motes danced in the long fingers of afternoon sunlight that fell on Sam's retreating figure. Odd how, even from this distance, the highlights that flickered in her black hair like tiny blue flames had the power to send waves of heat over his entire body.

As he watched her, she glanced back over her shoulder at him, then turned away quickly.

A.J.'s heart thundered in his chest. Even mad as hell, Sam could stir his blood like no other woman ever had.

He gave a snort of impatience with himself, then moved away from the window. He had to get a handle on this. The last thing he needed in his life was a woman, any woman, but especially not Samantha Ellis. Sam was the kind of woman who would settle down and make a home—a nester. She was exactly the type he seemed destined to get mixed up with, screw up their lives and his, then run from. Sam didn't deserve that.

What he needed to concentrate on was saving her life, not ruining it by hauling her into bed.

"She's going to give some poor, unsuspecting guy a run for his money."

At the sound of Santelli's voice, A.J. did a quick take of the fire chief's face. Santelli was also watching Sam move across the bay to the stairs. Was he interested in Sam? An electric charge of jealousy shot through him.

Santelli read his look, then smiled knowingly. "Don't worry. I'm not interested. I make it a policy not to get involved with women in my command. I've worked too hard to get where I am to throw it all away on a surge of testosterone." He leaned his forearms on the desk and stared at A.J. for a long moment before speaking again. "I know you haven't asked for this, but my advice is to steer a wide path around Sam. She's made it abundantly clear that a relationship with anyone is something she doesn't want any part of."

At first he thought the chief was teasing him, but Santelli looked as serious as a heart attack.

Had he been that transparent? A.J. avoided Santelli's gaze by reading the duty schedule posted on a corkboard beside the door. Unconsciously, he searched for Sam's name. When he found it, he read her schedule for the coming month. Then he felt Santelli's gaze still on him, and he quickly turned away.

He sat in the chair across from the chief, then laughed. The brittle sound made his next words ring hollow. "Don't worry, Joe. A relationship with Sam is the furthest thing from my mind. My only interest is to find out what's going on—and who's trying to kill her."

The next morning, unwilling to call A.J. as he'd instructed her to, Sam rented a car and drove herself to work. She had just settled at the hated desk in the corner of the apparatus bay when the phone rang. "Engine company one-oh-eight," she recited by rote with as much enthusiasm as she could muster, which on her personal can't-wait-to-do-it scale rated somewhere around minus one hundred.

"Sam?" Rachel Sutherland's concerned voice came over the wire. "A.J. and Luke told me what happened yesterday. Are you okay? Luke says Santelli put you on the duty desk."

Rachel's concern didn't surprise Sam, but it certainly raised her hackles at being reminded of her punishment, as if she needed reminding.

"I'm fine." With any luck that would be the end of this part of this conversation.

She'd suffered enough embarrassment over this. The guys hadn't stopped teasing her since the news got out. One of them even brought in a pillow for her to sit on.

More than a bit embarrassed at her situation, since her assignment would normally have been meted out to someone who had committed a serious infraction, Sam was miffed that A.J. had seen fit to spread the news of her embarrassment far and wide. Well, maybe that was an exaggeration, but Rachel would be one more person to point out to her that her life was in danger—a reminder she could do without and if she heard it one more time would send her running screaming from the room.

She knew that this was not a punishment, and that the chief and A.J. were only thinking of her safety. She should be thankful for that. But if it wasn't happening to her, it would be much easier. She could accept the logic of their actions. Still, being taken off active duty smarted and that A.J. had been instrumental in it really hurt. Then again, he had no idea how much firefighting meant to her.

Nor did he know how terrified she really was, and she would make sure he never found out. The very last thing she needed was A.J. hovering over her, protecting her, overseeing her every move. And he would. She knew that as surely as she knew her name.

"Are you sure?" Rachel said, cutting into her thoughts.

Good grief, had she said any of that out loud? "Sure about what?" With her mind centered on her troubles, Sam had lost the entire thread of her conversation with Rachel.

"Are you sure you're okay?" Rachel's voice had grown more tense.

Relieved that she hadn't voiced her thoughts, Sam rested her forehead in her hand. "Absolutely. I'm fine." Period.

Silence fell between them.

"So is that the only reason you called?" Sam asked, hoping to divert the conversation.

"No, but I promised Luke I wouldn't bring it up unless you're sure you're okay."

A sigh of impatience issued from her. "I've been through worse and lived to tell the tale, Rachel."

That wasn't entirely true. There had been only two other times in her life that Sam had felt this helpless, this defeated: when she was ten years old and her father had walked out of her life, and when she was nineteen and had to stand by and watch while her drunken mother was incinerated in a motel fire. Both times, she'd wondered if she would live through it. She had, but deep down, she still bore the scars. On top of that was her sister Karen's belief that Sam had stolen her childhood. Karen had cut off all communication with her, and she hadn't seen or talked to her only relative in too many years.

But she didn't want to think about any of that now. She had enough on her mind.

"Now that we've established that I'm not an emotional pile of mush, what was it you promised Luke you wouldn't bring up to me?" She tried to lace her voice with humor.

Rachel hesitated for a few seconds. "Well, okay, if you're sure. Actually, there are two things I wanted to talk to you about. The first is do you have a date for the children's burn unit charity ball next Saturday?"

Lately, with everything that had been going on, Sam hadn't given much thought to the ball. She wanted to go, but the only person she would want to go with was also the one person she was trying her best to avoid. Maybe she should just go alone. After all, nowadays that would hardly be looked down on. She laughed to herself. Like A.J. or Santelli would let that happen. If she wanted to go at all—and she did—then she'd find a date so she wouldn't have to listen to them.

"No, not yet, but I'm working on it," she finally told her friend, hoping it would put an end to the subject.

"Well, you better get a move on. It's coming up fast." Rachel paused. "Word is that a certain chief of detectives isn't spoken for yet." Before Sam could say anything, Rachel blurted, "FIST has a job. The man who owns the building that houses the Main Street bookstore that burned last week contacted me. They want us to investigate the fire for arson."

Sam came alert. She swung her swivel chair so her back was facing the main part of the bay. Suddenly, the depression she'd been carrying around since yesterday lifted. She was going to be unchained from the duty desk, and Santelli or A.J. could do nothing to prevent it. *Yes!*

Ever since the fire commissioners had sanctioned the Fire Investigation Special Team as an official branch of the department and she and Rachel had set up an office to do private investigations, it had been understood that their work took precedence and relieved Sam of her duties in the firehouse. The distraction of a job for FIST was just what the doctor ordered to lift her out of the doldrums. She loved doing the investigations with Rachel and had even given thought to leaving the fire company and working full-time for FIST.

"I thought the OGPD decided it wasn't arson." Sam held her breath waiting for Rachel's answer. If this was not arson, her butt would be planted in this desk chair for days to come.

"They did, but the owners think Bayside Insurance is—" Rachel's explanation was cut off by baby Jay crying in the background. "Maggie, please give Jay his pacifier for Mommy." The crying stopped. "Thanks, sweetie. Sorry about that, Sam. As I was saying, the owners think Bayside is trying to find a loophole to get out of paying a claim. The owner is willing to pay us to prove it's not arson."

An unsettling thought occurred to Sam. "Is FIST working this alone or are the police still involved?"

"We'll be doing it alone." A long, pregnant pause followed. "A.J. will be going with you, Sam. After what happened yesterday, it's the only way he and Luke would agree to letting you handle it."

Her stomach clenched. Even her best friend was supervising her life. Though she loved Rachel for it, she couldn't help resenting one more restriction being placed on her. She sighed.

If she were totally honest with herself, it wasn't the restrictions on her movements that bothered her. She understood the need for them and was even grateful. What set her nerves on edge was whom she'd be forced to be with. Would she ever get past this unreasonable attraction to A.J. if he popped up in her life every five minutes?

Maybe Rachel would go with her, or even Luke. Anyone but A.J. "Rach—"

The loud cry of a baby erupted once more. "Gotta run. Jay needs feeding. Just go over to the store with A.J. and nose around. I'll get the insurance company's report to him, and he'll get the building owner's permission tomorrow morning so you can get on the premises by afternoon. I'll meet with you here at our house tomorrow night to go over what you find. Seven okay?"

"Uh, yes, I guess so. But, Rach—"

"Good. See you then." The phone went dead.

Slowly, Sam swung her chair around and hung up the receiver. The good news was that thanks to the fire commissioners and a possible torch who had something against books, she'd be off the desk. The bad

news was she'd be spending more time with the one
man she didn't seem able to get out of her life or her
head.

But what about her heart?

Chapter 3

When Sam stepped from her rental car in front of the burned-out remains of the Written Word Bookstore the next afternoon, A.J. was already waiting. He'd just finished removing the wooden planks covering the doorway and was brushing off his hands. She couldn't drag her gaze from the muscles in his upper arms, which moved against the material of his light blue dress shirt and made her yearn to feel his arms around her. Her heartbeat sped up. Sam hadn't realized she'd been holding her breath until her chest began to ache.

Quickly, she sucked in air, gathered her equipment and boots from her trunk, slammed it shut and then exchanged her sneakers for the boots. After tossing her shoes into the car, she locked it and joined A.J. outside the front door of the bookstore.

During her years on the beauty pageant circuit as a child and later as a young adult, she'd met a lot of men. Never, in all that time, had she ever met one who could turn her into a big ball of sensuality as A.J. did, simply by standing there. She wasn't able to put her finger on it, but something about him reached out and touched her emotions in places that hadn't been touched in a very long time.

After her father had left, she'd locked up her heart to emotion. She thought she understood why he'd walked out on his family, but without knowing for sure, she couldn't find it in her heart to forgive him. Living with Sam's mother, who could only love Ben Franklin as he smiled back at her from a one-hundred-dollar bill, could not have been easy on her dad. Even today, every once in a while Sam would catch herself looking for his face in a crowd. Hoping he'd come back. Then she'd remember it had been eighteen years since she'd seen him. Would she recognize him after all this time? Was he even alive? Did she really care?

Only once after her father left had she allowed anyone in and that had been a huge mistake. Sloan Whitley had lied to her about having a wife and left her with nothing. But even Sloan hadn't had the hold on her emotions that A.J. seemed to have, and without even trying. God help her if he ever tried.

"Afternoon." A.J.'s deep voice roused her from her painful memories. He tried to take the heavy evidence case from her hand, but she resisted his help and retained a tight grip on the handle. Without argument, he stepped back. "You're right on time."

She'd have to take his word on that. Several times that morning she'd caught herself counting the minutes until she'd meet him. Only by taking off her watch and shoving it in her pocket had she been able to get a grip on herself.

"Let's get this show on the road," she said stiffly and stepped inside the burned carcass of what was once a quaint little bookstore. "Watch where you're walking so you don't inadvertently step on evidence," she called over her shoulder to A.J.

He knew the drill. Why did she find it necessary to remind him of the basic rules of fire investigation? Power, she told herself. She'd had so little of it over her life lately, it felt good to get back even that much, and that it was with him…

Though it had been a week since the bookstore's fire, the smell of wet, charred wood was still strong enough to make her catch her breath. Sam led the way through the debris of what remained of the building. Wood crunched beneath their feet. Puddles of water that hadn't yet completely evaporated sloshed black mud on the cuffs of their pants. Books, their pages burned and blackened, lay everywhere. A brown, mixed-breed dog rooted through the charred timbers, probably in hopes of finding some food. When his search turned up nothing, he cast them a wary glance, bounded over a sagging ceiling beam, then shot off down the street to renew his quest for nourishment.

They slipped on plastic gloves and went deeper into the front room of the building. Sam stared up at the only remaining interior wall.

"Hell of a mess," A.J. said, stopping beside her, his foot knocking against the aluminum evidence case she'd set on the floor at her feet.

While Sam did a quick check of the room, A.J. watched, his gaze shaking up her usual methodical efficiency. When she'd finished with her preliminary walk-through, he dug in his pocket and pulled out a piece of paper. "Rachel sent this insurance report over for us to use as a guide as to what their inspectors found." For a moment, he scanned the report, then looked around. He pointed toward a window with the glass missing. "The inspector said he thought maybe a thief or an arsonist came through that broken window. We didn't agree."

Sam walked over to just below it, shoved some of the debris on the floor aside with her shovel and then sighed. "This is a no-brainer. Either the inspector did this blindfolded, or he's just plain stupid. There's no glass on the floor around the window. A first-year fire academy probie would know that if someone broke in, there would be glass all over the floor. My guess is the heat blew the window out." She straightened and looked at A.J. "Did they find glass outside?"

A.J. glanced at the police report. "Yes, and according to the investigating officer, enough to make up the missing window."

Sam shook her head. "I'm surprised the insurance company didn't catch that. Then again, maybe it served their purpose to overlook the obvious. Wouldn't be the first time. You get an owner who doesn't know and they can pull anything on them to keep from having to write a big settlement check."

She glanced at A.J. He grimaced and nodded knowingly. Then he smiled. Her stomach did a crazy flip.

If all the so-called proof was as flimsy as this, they'd be out of here before her hormones had a chance to embarrass her, and she'd be heading back to the desk, which, although she hated it, was a far safer prospect than spending the afternoon with A.J. But as long as he kept his distance, she was fairly certain she could handle her hormone eruption. "What else does the insurance report say?"

He scanned it again. "There's a note here about frayed wires in an electrical outlet behind the counter."

Sam slid behind the partially burned divider. She inspected the wiring inside an electrical outlet box dangling from the wall. The coating on the wire wasn't melted. Since fire didn't damage unexposed wiring, she had to assume the electrical box was removed after the fire.

As she checked the wire, she felt A.J. squat beside her. Instantly, her nerve endings came to life. She dropped the wire. A.J. was pressing lightly against her. A tingle raced down her side. She wanted to move away, but with all the debris that had been torn from the walls by the firefighters, she couldn't move without pushing him backward.

She took a deep breath, then curled her nose against the musty odor of burned materials that had been wet, then grown moldy in the Florida heat. She turned her head slightly. Instead of the musty smell, she encountered the smell of a man: woodsy, rugged and way too virile for her peace of mind. Waves of desire washed over her, nearly swamping her with their intensity. She struggled to keep her head above the emotional flood waters.

"So, is the wiring the culprit?" A.J. hadn't looked at her. Instead he remained squatting beside her with his pen poised above his notebook to make notations. "It doesn't look bad."

Thankful that he had unwittingly released a bit of his emotional hold on her, Sam reached for the wire to show him the lack of evidence of fire damage, but instead of grabbing wiring, she grabbed warm, masculine fingers. A.J.'s.

Electricity, so strong she wondered if the outlet were live, shot up her arm. She closed her eyes against the yearning that was building inside her. It swelled and threatened to erupt. She couldn't let anything happen. She couldn't. She had to be strong. Fight it. She had to—

Then she felt his thumb drawing small, slow circles on the back of her hand. The electricity returned, shooting to all points of her body, bringing them to life in a way she had never experienced, even with Sloan. She tried to pull away, but he tightened his hold.

In a last-ditch effort to stop what seemed inevitable, Sam made a feeble attempt to force him to halt. "A.J....I...we...you... Don't—"

"Why, Sam? We both want it." His breath feathered her face, warm and sweet. His mouth... Lord, help her, his mouth. It was so close, so very close. So tempting, so—

She closed her eyes.

Then it happened. A.J. was kissing her, and she was kissing him back with all the pent-up desire she'd buried inside her. She knew she should be fighting, but all common sense had been swamped by the heat coursing through her. And suddenly, she didn't want it to stop. She wanted more, much more.

Then he was gone, and she found herself cold and empty. She could hear him on the other side of the counter. He was pacing, and she could imagine him raking his fingers through his hair. From the sound of his hurried footsteps, the kiss had shaken him as much as it had her.

Slowly but surely, she gathered her wits about her and, even more slowly, the deluge of conflicting hot flashes and chills brought on by the devastating kiss faded. Her heart rhythm slowed.

When she had herself under control again and felt as if she could face him, she crawled from behind the counter, then straightened. "I guess we can leave. We've done all we can do here."

As soon as the words passed her lips, she realized the suggestiveness they inadvertently transmitted. Her gaze shot to A.J.

He smiled. "Not quite."

Instantly, her pulse rate accelerated.

A.J. steered the car into his designated slot in the parking lot of the OGPD, where he finally allowed himself to think about what had just happened with Sam at the bookstore. He licked his lips and could still taste her on them. His fist doubled up and pain shot through his arm. Only then did he realize he'd slammed his hand against the steering wheel. With a long sigh, he laid his head back against the headrest.

What the hell were you thinking?

And there lay the crux of the entire situation. He *hadn't* been thinking, not with his head anyway. If he had, he wouldn't have kissed her. Problem was, when he got that close to Sam, his brain shut down, and his body took over his thinking process. That offer of a job with the BCI was looking better all the time.

Worst of it was, he still had to face Sam later that night at Luke and Rachel's. He picked up his cell phone, intent on calling Rachel and telling her he couldn't make it. Before he'd punched in the last number, he snapped the phone closed and squeezed it in his fist.

He was many things, but he wasn't a coward. He'd go, and he'd face Sam. Hopefully, he wouldn't do anything else that could be added to his stupid-things-I-did-today list.

Even in the dark, Sam never had a problem finding Rachel's house. She'd recently taken up gardening as a hobby, and her flowers were the most profuse and prettiest on the entire street. As Sam pulled into the driveway of the Sutherlands' house, she noted a vehicle parked in the shadow of the house beside Luke's pickup. She got out of her car and, as she rounded the bumper of the pickup, she recognized the other vehicle as the same make and model that A.J. drove.

Involuntarily, her heart rate sped up. She paused in the driveway. Had Rachel said he'd be there and had Sam pushed it from her mind so she wouldn't have to deal with it? Did she want to see him after the kiss at the bookstore? What would she say? Calling herself every kind of a coward, she decided to act as if nothing had happened. After all, what good would come of bringing it up and embarrassing both of them in front of Luke and Rachel?

If she'd known he'd be here, she would have dressed differently, but it was too late to change that now. At the front door, she tugged on the cuffs of her white linen shorts and adjusted the pink camisole top to cover most of her midriff. Satisfied she looked presentable, she pushed the doorbell half-hidden beneath a spray of dried flowers hanging on the door frame. Seconds after she heard the chime echoing inside, the door flew open.

"Aunt Sam!" Maggie cried and threw herself at her.

Over the child's head, Sam could see Rachel watching them closely from midway down the hall. Though Maggie was doing better, Rachel still hadn't gotten over her being kidnapped and kept a vigilant eye on her child.

Missing from Rachel and Luke's daughter's arms was the patchwork teddy bear that had been her lifeline during the time she'd been the captive of arsonist and kidnapper Charlene Daniels. When she'd given up possession of the bear to her baby brother Jay, it had heralded a big milestone in Maggie's psychological recovery from her ordeal.

Over a year had passed since Maggie had been returned to her mother and father. With the help of a very good child psychologist, she was rapidly turning into a happy little girl again. Rarely did any of them glimpse a shadow of the silent child who'd been taken from her parents' apartment, kept for two years as the arsonist's child, then found in Daniels's bedroom closet.

Sam leaned over, engulfed the little girl in a tight hug, then planted a loud kiss on her cheek. "Hey, angel. Where's your dad?" she asked, tucking one of Maggie's blond braids over her shoulder.

"He's in the living room." Maggie latched on to Sam's hand, giving her just enough time to close the front door before pulling her into the entry hall. Before Sam could take a breath, Maggie had hauled her into the living room. "Uncle Jay's here, too," she announced as they crossed the threshold.

Sam stopped dead. *Uncle Jay* was Maggie's name for A.J. She'd been hoping he was in the garage with Luke tinkering with the car or something so she'd have a little prep time before she had to face him. However, by the time the words had passed through Maggie's lips, Sam found herself staring straight into A. J. Branson's mesmerizing blue eyes.

Good God!

It had been hard enough ignoring the man in a business suit. Seeing him in body-hugging jeans that outlined all his male attributes, and a muscle-defining T-shirt, she'd be lucky if she didn't melt into a puddle right in the middle of Rachel's brand-new beige carpeting. To draw breath, she had to give it conscious thought. His lips, the ones that had expertly claimed hers that very afternoon with a possessiveness that, in retrospect, scared her, were curved in a smile. Heat suffused her body, making her grateful for her brief attire.

Sam dragged her gaze from A.J. to Rachel, who was standing in the circle of Luke's protective arm grinning like a delighted child who had just pulled off something on her parents. *Great.* Give the woman one little glimmer of an idea and she takes it upon herself to build it into a matchmaking mountain.

Sam threw Rachel a look that said she'd deal with her later, then turned back to A.J. Their eyes met and once more, all the sensations she'd experienced that afternoon in the bookstore came rushing back. She fought for control.

"Evening," she said, her voice forced and formal.

A.J.'s thick brows furrowed over his captivating Nordic blue eyes. "Nice to see you, too." His deep voice rolled over Sam like ocean waves washing over a sandy beach. The man's charm just oozed out of his pores. A.J., she decided, should be declared harmful to any woman's mental health, especially hers.

"What are you doing here?" Sam blurted at A.J.

He stared at her for a long time, then lowered his voice to a faint whisper. "Sam, about this afternoon, I—"

"Don't worry about it. It was nothing," she bit out before he could say more. "Nothing."

A.J.'s mouth snapped shut. His brows furrowed into that frown that she knew meant he was not happy. The two of them remained in the middle of the floor glaring at each other. She stood her ground, but she had a sneaky suspicion that he didn't believe her, that he knew that kiss had rocked her world and that it had taken her a good part of the afternoon to get her feet back under her.

Rachel stepped out of her husband's sheltering embrace. "Okay, kiddies." Rachel inserted herself between them. "Now that we've all exchanged cordial hellos…" Taking Sam's arm, she led her to the couch. "Let's sit down and chat, shall we? Luke, Sam needs a drink."

Luke smiled. "What's it gonna be?" He winked at Sam, and his conspiratorial grin matched Rachel's in exuberance.

Terrific! An ambush. Sam glared at him. "How about hemlock for two?" She looked pointedly from Luke to his wife.

Luke laughed and headed for the bar along one wall. He lifted a bottle of clear liquid for her to see. "Gin and tonic?"

Sam nodded. Then, leaning close to Rachel's ear, she warned between clenched teeth, "First chance I get, I am going to seriously maim both of you."

Rachel tossed Sam a playful smirk, as if she'd just complimented her on her shade of lipstick, then steered her around the glass-topped coffee table to a tropical turquoise sofa. "Please, not in front of the child," she whispered, then she gripped Sam's arm tighter to get her attention. "It won't kill you to be nice. You might even be able to finally admit that you like him." She smiled sweetly and left Sam sitting awkwardly on the edge of the sofa, then took a seat in a wicker chair with turquoise and mauve cushions that faced Sam. A.J. stood to one side. "Why don't you sit by Sam, A.J.?"

Sam ground her teeth. Rachel had no idea what she was doing. Like him? How she wished it was as simple as that. She looked longingly at the door. But she knew she would have to either sit here quietly or make a scene. Reluctantly Sam scooted over to make plenty of room for A.J.

Trying not to show the reluctance he felt, A.J. slid onto the sofa. When Rachel had stopped by his office to make sure he'd be at the meeting, he'd confirmed that he would and had looked at it as an opportunity to apologize to Sam for what had happened in the bookstore. Now that he was here and Sam was here, A.J. would have felt more comfortable sitting on a burning stick of dynamite.

It took every ounce of willpower he had to keep his gaze off that little top, which clung to her like a second skin as it flashed sections of her bare midriff at him, and Sam's endlessly long, tanned legs, the longest legs he'd ever seen on such a petite woman. Sweat broke out on his forehead despite the air-conditioning in the house.

He quickly averted his gaze to the toe of one of his scruffy sneakers. This was going to be a very long night.

Luke brought Sam her drink and gave A.J. a fresh bottle of beer. Fighting the urge to down the entire contents, he sipped at it instead. As Luke walked past on his way to sit on the arm of Rachel's chair, the breeze from his passing wafted a hint of Sam's soft, flowery perfume to A.J. His groin tightened. He pulled the throw pillow from behind him and laid it casually on his lap.

"Now, Mommy? Can I ask now?" Maggie begged Rachel.

Lovingly, Rachel brushed a strand of blond hair off Maggie's cheek. "Yes, baby. You *may* ask now."

"Aunt Sam?" Maggie said, sidling up to Sam. "Will you come to my birthday party Sunday after next Sunday?"

Sam frowned as if doing a quick calculation of Maggie's time frame. "Wouldn't miss it for anything. Let's see now," she said, appearing to be deep in thought, "what kind of present do I get for someone who's gonna be twenty-nine?"

Maggie's face grew concerned. "Aunt Sam, I'm only gonna be seven."

Sam laughed and hugged her. "My mistake. You look so much older."

When she let go, Maggie stepped back, her blue eyes dancing with excitement. "Mommy and Daddy are taking me to swim with the dolphins, and then we're gonna have a birthday picnic. We're gonna have cake and deviled eggs and hot dogs and balloons and—" The child took a fast breath. "Uncle Jay's coming, too."

A.J. watched as Sam's smile melted as fast as ice cream on a hot day, then was quickly replaced by one obviously forced for the child's benefit. "Of course, I'll have to check to make sure that I don't have to work."

"Oh, please, Aunt Sam. Please. It won't be any fun without you."

A.J. silently agreed.

"Well, we'll see." Sam chucked her under the chin.

A pang of disappointment arrowed through A.J. She was trying to back out because he'd be there. Then he recalled something.

Nice try, Sam, but you're not gonna wiggle off the hook that easy.

"You don't have to work that Sunday," he said.

Pink flooded her cheeks. "Oh? How do you know?"

He grinned. "I saw the duty schedule in Santelli's office."

She glared at him for a moment, then turned to Maggie with a smile. "Well, then, I guess you can count me in."

"Yippee," Maggie yelled. "Aunt Sam's coming, too, Daddy."

"Yes, we heard, and I'm sure everyone in the neighborhood did as well." Luke looked at his daughter as if she were the most important thing on earth. "Okay, Magpie, time for bed," Luke said.

Maggie frowned. "Aw, Daddy. Can't I stay up just a little more time?"

"Bed," her mother repeated more firmly. "We said you could stay up long enough to invite Aunt Sam. You've done that, so now, it's time to say good night." Rachel waited patiently while Maggie reluctantly hugged and kissed A.J. and Sam, prolonging each endearment as long as possible.

A sinking sensation invaded A.J.'s stomach as he watched both Luke and Rachel disappear down the hall with their daughter, leaving him and Sam alone. He suddenly felt as if the rug had been pulled out from under him. Why did this woman have the power to make him feel like a kid fresh out of the tenth grade on his first date?

Sam sighed.

"Bored?" he asked for lack of anything else to say.

She looked at him and shook her head. "No, just

thinking. I was kind of hoping they'd have a regular birthday party for Maggie. You know, the kind with lots of kids, balloons, ice cream, noisemakers, a clown and all the regular kid stuff."

"Sounds as if you've been to a few of these shindigs yourself."

Her blue eyes lost their sparkle, and she turned away. "No. I've never been to a birthday party."

A.J. frowned. Surely she had been to a birthday party sometime in her life. "Not even your own?"

Sam shook her head, then rose and went to the bar. "Especially not my own." Busying herself by adding ice to her glass, she avoided his gaze. "The Tiny Tots beauty pageant in Phoenix was on my birthday every year, so there was never time. Besides, my mother thought birthday parties were a waste of money."

He cringed at the sadness that tinged her voice. "So, you were a child beauty queen, huh?" Why hadn't he known that? But then there was so much about Sam he didn't know. So much he wanted to know. Like everything that had happened to her from the time she left the birth canal to when she'd walked into Rachel's living room tonight.

As she walked back to the sofa, she tucked a stray hair back into the knot at the base of her neck. His fingers itched to release the confining hairdo and watch the night-black strands fall over her shoulders while he—

"That was my other life," she said. "One that I gave up when I stowed the trophies and certificates in my spare-room closet." She took a long gulp of her drink, then glanced anxiously down the hall where Luke and Rachel had disappeared. "Can we talk about something else?"

"Sure." The conversation about her childhood may have ended, but A.J. could see by the frown lines between her eyes that she had not stopped thinking about it.

A pain cut across his heart for the woman whose childhood consisted of nothing more than a few trophies and certificates stuck away in a closet. But mostly it ached for the little girl who had never blown out candles on her own cake, never taken part in a game of Pin the Tail on the Donkey, never dove into stacks of presents while her excited friends looked on. How many other things had she missed out on because her mother had evidently never considered the importance of having a childhood?

Sam squirmed under A.J.'s watchful gaze from across Rachel's dining-room table. She added her empty cake plate to the stack Rachel was collecting. After depositing them in the sink, Rachel refilled Sam's coffee cup. Adding cream and sugar, Sam stirred the light brown liquid and tried to block out thoughts of that kiss she and A.J. had shared that kept popping into her head every time she looked at him. If she allowed herself, she could still feel how warm and sweet that kiss had been. How her heart had cried out for him to take her in his arms and never let go. How—

She blinked away the daydream and checked her watch. "It's getting late. Can we get down to the reason

for this little gathering?" she asked, hoping to distract
A.J. and get this evening over with.

Rachel laid a manila folder in front of them. "Sam's
right. We need to talk FIST business," she announced.
"What did you two find at the bookstore?"

In the year since Rachel and Sam had founded FIST,
they had investigated several arson sprees, a serial
arsonist and at least a dozen insurance fires. Though
they'd started slow, word was rapidly spreading around
the state that if a fire chief or an insurance company had
a fire that required special investigation, they called
FIST.

"This was an easy one," Sam said, brushing a strand
of hair from her cheek.

"What do you know about Bayside Insurance?"
A.J. asked.

"Rachel?" Luke looked at his wife.

Rachel opened the folder and scanned it. "They're an
old company that was absorbed into the Florida Life and
Property Company. When they merged, most of the
Bayside employees were pensioned off and the
company installed their own people in the jobs. According to this, their business has been less than stellar this
year. I think the bookstore was a tax write-off and they
needed the deduction, so…" She frowned at Sam and
A.J. "Why?"

"Because A.J. and I think the insurance company is
trying to get out of paying. There's no evidence of arson
there. I went over the outlet wiring that they claimed
might have started it, and there's no evidence of it. The
window they said was broken into was blown *out* by the

heat, not *in* by any intruder." She glanced at A.J. then looked away. "I checked around the store for the point of origin and found a water leak in the back wall, right above the circuit breakers. The wall above it was black. Textbook V Burn mark. Bottom line is, these guys don't want to cough up the settlement check."

Rachel had been taking notes while Sam talked. "Well, that's going to make our clients very happy. You took pictures, right?" Sam nodded. Rachel collected Sam and A.J.'s written reports and added them to her folder. "That's about it then. I'll call the bookstore owner tomorrow."

Quickly, before Rachel could find an excuse for her to stay, Sam rose to make her exit. She'd had about all of A.J.'s sexual aura she could take for one night. "Well, I'm gonna hit the road. Thanks for everything," she said, making her way to the door.

"Good night," Rachel and Luke called as she hurried out of the air-conditioned house and into the humid Florida night.

Without turning, she waved at them over her shoulder.

"I'll walk you to your car," a deep voice said from just behind her.

She spun and came face-to-face with A.J. "Ah, thanks, but I'll be fine."

"That wasn't a question, Sam." Her name rolled off his tongue like a caress after a night of hot sex. She shivered and fought to keep her equilibrium.

Leaving her no room for argument, he took her arm gently in his grasp and steered her down the driveway to her car. The nearly moonless night closed in on them, creating an intimate atmosphere that Sam—with A.J.'s

warm fingers still wrapped around her upper arm—
found way too confining. She tried to pull free, but his
grip tightened just enough to prevent her escape.

Halfway down the front walk, he pulled her to a
standstill. "Unlock the car."

She looked at him, then remembered that unlocking
her SUV had been the trigger for the bomb. Without a
word, she hit the remote. The lights on the car flashed,
and they could hear the distinctive *click* of the door
locks releasing.

"Okay, let's go." A.J. pushed her forward.

When they reached her car, he held her away while
he looked into the backseat. Only when he was sure it
was safe did he release her.

She turned and, before she could express her thanks,
she found herself pinned up against the cold fender,
staring straight into the eyes of the first man who had
brought her blood to a rolling boil since Sloan Whitley.
No, she corrected, Sloan had never made her feel as if
her body had all the rigidity of cooked spaghetti and as
if her head were filled with helium.

As A.J.'s face moved closer to hers, she stared at his
mouth, full and tempting.

He's going to kiss me. I have to stop him. I have to…

Any warnings her brain sent her vanished, burned to
ashes with the invading heat, leaving behind only a
deep longing to feel his lips pressed against hers again.

"I was going to apologize for kissing you today,"
he growled, his voice low and sultry, "but I decided
that would be hypocritical." He lowered his mouth
toward hers.

Chapter 4

Sam held her breath in anticipation of a repeat of the wild rush of desire she'd experienced the last time A.J. had kissed her. Though she tried to clear her mind and fight him, she was failing miserably. His warm breath heated her skin. His aftershave drugged her senses, willing her to surrender herself to this man who had become far too important in her life.

His mouth was coming closer. Sam's blood pressure skyrocketed.

"Wait!"

Sam and A.J. sprang apart like two teenagers caught necking in the back of the classroom.

For a moment, Sam's blurry mind thought the interruption had come from her, but then it registered that it wasn't her voice. Rachel had broken the spell. Thankfully, A.J. moved in front of her, giving her a few seconds to clear the cotton wool of passion from her wayward senses before facing her friend.

Once she had the sexual magnetism under control, or as under control as she could get it with A.J. so close, Sam stepped around him and saw Rachel standing on the front porch, a knowing smile curving her lips. Damn her! Sam promised herself a long talk with her matchmaking friend the next day. This whole thing with A.J. was hard enough without Rachel's interference.

"Sorry." Sam knew Rachel wasn't sorry at all. Her expression was one of pure delight. "I just wanted to remind you, Sam, that you still need to get a date for the burn unit ball next Saturday. You, too, A.J.," she added, emphasizing *too*.

As if Sam could forget with Rachel calling it to her attention daily. "I know. I'll take care of it."

She could feel A.J. stir beside her. Glancing up at him, she noted he was staring down at her with concentrated interest, as if trying to make up his mind about something. Then his expression changed.

He smiled.

Sam gasped. If she was reading the intent written plainly in his eyes, then he was about to ask her to be his date. He opened his mouth to speak.

"Well…I'm…gonna run." She quickly sidestepped him, jumped in her car, slammed the door and was off down the street in a flash. In her review mirror, she could see Rachel on the porch and A.J. standing open-mouthed on the curb.

Having made her escape, she flipped the AC to high

to combat the aftereffects of the almost-kiss. The chilly air had no sooner begun to cool her heated skin than her questioning mind clicked into gear. Would A.J. show up at the firehouse tomorrow to ask her to go with him? If she knew nothing else about this man, A. J. Branson's determination mirrored that of a seasoned bloodhound. One of the many things that made him such a great cop.

But right now, she didn't need a good cop. What she needed was a date—and not with A. J. Branson. It didn't take a genius to figure out that if she couldn't spend fifteen minutes with him in a dirty, burned-out building without falling into his arms, she would never survive an entire evening in the intimate confines of a dance floor. That scenario posed possibilities Sam didn't even want to contemplate. Somehow, between now and tomorrow morning, she had to find a date.

"I don't even know how to dance, Sam. I'm only going for the kids and because I'm expected to be there."

Sam almost laughed out loud. Joe Santelli, a fire-fighter who had faced any number of life-threatening situations and could stare down the best of his tough firefighters, looked scared to death at the prospect of having to dance with her or anyone.

"So go with me, Chief. I promise, you won't have to dance. This will be a purely platonic date. Once we get there, you can go your way, and I'll go mine until it's time to go home."

He stared at her for a long, intense moment, as if his decision would effect the rotation of the earth. "Why *me?*" he finally said.

Sam hesitated. She couldn't very well tell him the real reason was to avoid A.J. "To get Rachel Sutherland off my back." Not entirely false. "She's been harassing me to get a date and until I do, she's not going to let it rest." She put on her best pleading face. "What do you say? Will you do it?"

"Why don't you just go alone?"

She stared at him for a bit then laughed derisively. "As if after all that's happened in the last few days, you and A.J. would let that happen."

He paced his office for a moment, then dropped into his desk chair. For another moment or two he fiddled with a pen. "Okay, but you better be telling me the truth about no dancing."

His agreement washed the tension from her body that had taken up residence the night before in front of Rachel's house.

"Two left feet?" she asked, smiling broadly.

"More like six." He grinned sheepishly. "I can supervise a fire in a high-rise apartment building, but I can't master the simplest dance step. Never could. I was born without coordination."

"Well," she said, willing to let him off the hook, "I promise I won't test you on that. No dancing." She started to leave, then turned back to him. "Thanks a million, Chief. I owe you one."

"You bet you do." He laughed.

Sam was heading to her car when she met A.J. coming up the walk to the firehouse.

"I was just coming to talk to you," he said.

She knew it. Thank goodness she'd read him right and gotten to Joe before A.J. showed up. "Oh? What for?" she asked guilelessly.

Two firefighters arriving for the shift change came toward them. A.J. took her elbow and steered her onto the grass beneath one of the towering palms on the front lawn. The old man on the bench across the street followed their movements with unusual interest. An inexplicable shiver skidded up Sam's spine.

"You're not cold, are you?" A.J. looked at her as if she were crazy to be cold in heat that had to be hitting the mid-to-high nineties.

She pulled her gaze from the old man and shook her head. He was probably just someone who lived in the neighborhood. She saw the same people pass by here every day. He shouldn't be any different. Yet he bothered her. Residue from everything that had happened lately? Until now, she hadn't realized how much recent events were unconsciously coloring the way she looked at those around her.

No, she told herself. You can't start imagining that everyone you see is trying to kill you. If you do, you'll make yourself nuts. Just lead your life as usual.

"No. Just a sudden chill. I guess someone walked over my grave, as my mother used to say." Unable to stop herself, she glanced across the street. The bench was empty, the man nowhere in sight. See? He is probably no more threatening than the bench on which he sat. Get a grip!

Dragging her attention back to A.J., she forced a smile. "So what did you want to talk to me about?"

"Saturday night. The ball."

Sam swallowed. Now that she had to turn him down, she felt a stab of unreasonable regret.

Good God, Sam, make up your mind. Either you want to go with him or you don't. Which is it?

It wasn't that she didn't want to go with A.J. She just didn't dare. Going with him on a date, any date, would put more at risk than Sam was willing to gamble.

"What about it?" she asked, playing dumb. Deep inside she hated herself for the deceit she'd pulled off on A.J., but her first priority was her peace of mind. If it took a few white lies and a little masquerading to get it, then so be it. She could not allow her guard to drop when it came to A.J.

Now that he was in front of Sam, A.J. felt like a kid asking a girl to go to their first prom. He took a deep breath and blurted out the words before he could change his mind. "Will you go with me?"

She looked at the ground. "I'm sorry, A.J. I'm going with Joe."

He felt as if he'd just taken a blow to his midsection. "Santelli?" He recalled Santelli's assurance that he had no personal interest in Sam. Had he lied to him? Jealousy as green as the grass on which they stood flooded through him.

She nodded.

"But last night—"

"The arrangements were made this morning."

A.J. ran his hand through his hair. He didn't know which feeling coursing through him was the strongest: anger, jealousy or disappointment. Whatever it was, he wasn't about to stand here and further embarrass himself. He turned on his heel and strode angrily to his car.

Sam put the finishing touch on her upswept hairdo, fluffed the curls framing her face and stepped back to check her full reflection in her bedroom mirror. The plain black gown she'd chosen, with its deep-cut neckline and open back, had been on sale and was just right for tonight. It clung to her slight figure like a glove, accentuating the curve of her hip and the swell of her braless breasts. A single pearl hanging from a fine gold chain lay against her cleavage and large gold hoops hung from her earlobes.

"Not bad, Ellis," she said, twisting and turning while she studied her reflection. "Not bad at all."

The doorbell sounded.

"That must be your date," she told the woman smiling at her from the mirror. She gave herself one more check, smoothed the fabric of her gown over her hips and nodded in approval.

Since A.J. didn't have a date, he probably wouldn't be coming to the ball, so she was looking forward to a pleasant evening free of the sexual tension that had dogged her like a persistent specter for the past few days. Tonight, Samantha Ellis was going to have fun and damn A. J. Branson.

Quickly, she grabbed her small, beaded evening purse and a black shawl laced with gold threads and headed for the front door. After checking through the peephole in her new door and assuring herself it was

Joe, she flung the door open and gasped. Standing on the threshold was a man she'd never seen before—Joe Santelli in black tie and looking like he just stepped out of a James Bond movie.

"If I may say so, sir, you sure clean up real nice," she said.

Santelli acted as if he hadn't heard her. Instead he just stood there, gawking. That he found her transformation from firefighter to woman acceptable pleased Sam, but she couldn't help wishing it was A.J. standing on her doorstep being bowled over by the change, and not the chief of Engine Company 108.

"Chief?" She waved her hand in front of his face. "Joe?"

He blinked. "Uh, yeah." He swallowed hard. "Geez, Sam, you could have given a guy some warning."

"Warning?" she asked innocently.

Joe noted her mischievous grin, then shook his head. "Get in the car."

With her spirits light and her nerves more relaxed than they'd been in days, Sam laughed. "Yes, sir."

The Palms Hotel and Resort's uniformed parking attendant leaned down to see inside Joe's car. "Sir, please back into the parking space. It will make for an easier departure when you get ready to leave."

Joe nodded and proceeded to maneuver his car into the space the attendant indicated. While he did so, Sam checked the well-lit lot for A.J.'s car. When she didn't see it, a wave of disappointment washed over her. She shook herself and reminded that rebellious part of her that it was a good thing that A.J. had decided not to come. She could relax and enjoy the evening.

"Let's go," she heard Joe say, and realized she'd been so busy searching for A.J.'s car, she hadn't even heard Joe exit the driver's side and come around and open her door. Now, he stood beside her, his hand out to assist her. She took it, and they walked toward the entrance and into the lobby. A large sign on an easel told them that the 25th Annual Children's Burn Unit Ball was in the Flagler Ballroom.

When they entered the expansive room, Sam felt as if she'd stepped into a fairy tale. The ballroom glittered with tiny white lights and resounded with the voices of the two hundred fashionably attired guests milling about or gliding around the dance floor to the twenty-piece orchestra.

Nervously, she scanned the faces, looking for one in particular. Despite her vow to have fun, the moment she stepped through the doors, she'd felt her stomach tighten and her nerves go on alert. She didn't see A.J. While that didn't mean he wasn't there, some of the tension drained from her.

Joe escorted her to one of the many elegantly set tables circled around the highly polished dance floor. "Drink?"

"Please." She smiled up at him. "Gin and tonic."

Joe grinned. "You sure you don't want one of the fancy drinks with the umbrellas?"

"I gave up those fluffy drinks a long time ago." About the same time she had given up the beauty pageant circuit, she thought. "Gin and tonic will be fine."

He hurried off and disappeared into the crowd around the bar that had been set up at the far end of the room. She couldn't help but wonder if he was just making sure she'd hold to her agreement not to make him dance.

The orchestra was playing a slow, dreamy number and Sam got caught up in the moment. She looked around, admiring the designer gowns and the expensive jewels.

"Samantha?" The voice was a woman's, and it came from directly behind her. She swung around to find Kevin's mother, Marcia Hilary, standing beside Henry Donaldson, the fire commissioner. Marcia was dressed in a pure white lace evening gown, her hennaed hair swept up in curls on the top of her head. Diamonds dripped from her ears and hung around her chickenlike neck.

She stood. "Mrs. Hilary. Commissioner."

"Please, call me Marcia." The woman smiled and tightened her hand around the upper arm of the man beside her.

"Would you like to join Chief Santelli and me?" Sam asked, motioning to the empty chairs at her table.

"You came with Santelli?" the commissioner asked.

"Yes. Neither of us had a date, so it seemed the best answer for both of us." Why was she so eager to make sure they knew Santelli and she had no romantic connection? She didn't have time to delve for an answer.

"I'm afraid we can't join you, dear, I just came over to ask you to add your name to the list of ladies in the bachelorette auction." She flashed her most manipulative smile, the same smile Sam had seen her use on her son, and waved a small notebook, one page of which held several names already.

A feeling of intense dread invaded Sam's good mood. She shook her head. People buying the company of a woman reminded her too much of the dog and pony shows that had dominated her childhood. "I don't think so."

Marcia looked up at her escort, her full mouth puckering into a pout. "Henry, talk to her. If you order her to do it, she'd have to obey, wouldn't she?"

The commissioner patted her hand. "I'm afraid not, dear." Then he turned to Sam. "This is for charity, Ms. Ellis. For the children. All you'd have to do is dance once with the man who bids the highest for you. That's it."

For the children. They sure knew how to grab Sam by the heart. Still, the idea of stepping on a stage again… She was being foolish. How long would it take for the bidding? Minutes. She could be off the stage in minutes. "Okay. I guess that wouldn't be too bad." Just then Kevin showed up. "Hi, Kevin."

"Hello, Sam," he said, then looked at his mother. Sam detected the usual nervous posture Kevin always assumed around this woman.

"Samantha has agreed to let us auction her off, Kevin." Marcia smiled that saccharine smile of hers.

"Great!" Kevin stuck his hands in his pockets and shifted nervously from one foot to the other.

"Kevin, do stop fidgeting, dear, and get Mother a drink." She grinned at him, but Sam felt her request was very insincere. It didn't seem as if she wanted a drink, but more that she wanted to get rid of her son. When he didn't move, she added sharply, "Now, Kevin."

"Yes, Mother." Kevin cast an embarrassed glance at Sam, then hurried off in the same direction Joe had gone earlier.

Sam wanted to tell Marcia to treat the poor kid like an adult and not her lackey, but she bit it back.

Once more that stiff smile twisted Marcia's lips. She jotted something in her notebook. "We'll be starting the auction in about five or ten minutes, so be ready to come up on the stage when I call your name." She wiggled the tips of her fingers at Sam. "See you in a few."

Already regretting that she'd agreed, Sam nodded and watched as the commissioner led Marcia toward the stage. Her stomach began that slow, painful churning it had always started before she walked on a pageant stage.

The first girl to be auctioned off, Susan Clark, a stunning blonde with a blinding white smile, looked very pleased to be ogled by every man in the room. Sam wished that she could take this as casually as Ms. Clark did. She knew that standing on that stage was going to bring to life memories of other stages, memories she fought daily to keep hidden inside herself. Sam's turn came all too soon.

"Our next bachelorette is Samantha Ellis, one of Orange Grove's brave firefighters," Marcia announced.

Very slowly, Sam stood and made her way to the foot of the stairs leading up to the stage. Physically forcing herself to do it, she put her foot on the first step, then the second, and the third, until she stood in the glaring spotlight. This was the part she hated the most about the beauty pageants. After her father left, every time she'd stepped on a stage, terror had accosted her like a hungry monster, eating away her confidence and making her limbs quake.

Sweat broke out on her palms. She curled her fingers, plastered a smile on her lips and told herself over and over that this would end very soon.

"As you can see, gentlemen, she doesn't look like the typical firefighter who rescues stranded cats from trees." Marcia's voice seemed to come to her from far away. "It would appear that our firefighter can brave a blaze, but standing up here has given her a slight case of stage fright."

Sam felt fingers close over her bare arm and urge her farther into the blinding light.

"What is the bid for this brave young lady?"

A man's voice came from Sam's right. "One hundred dollars."

"I have one hundred dollars, but I'm sure you can do better than that for the children," Marcia announced, a pout coloring her voice. "Do I have two?"

"Two," came another voice from the left of the stage.

"Five," another voice yelled before Marcia could register the last bid.

The heat in the room intensified. The odor of perfume filled Sam's nostrils. The room began to spin slowly. Sam's stomach heaved. She swallowed, refusing to get sick in front of all these people.

It will be over soon, she told herself as she often had

as a child. *Hang on. Just a few more minutes.* Her stomach rumbled threateningly. *Oh, God, please make it fast.*

The faces in the crowd beyond the stage blurred, and the voices rose to an almost deafening volume.

"One thousand dollars." The bid came from somewhere at the back of the room.

Chapter 5

A.J. had only just arrived when the bachelorette auction began. When Marcia had called Sam to the stage and he got his first glimpse of her, his mouth had gone dry and every nerve ending in his body had come to attention. *Beautiful* was a pale description of Sam in that black gown, even though he knew her beauty went far deeper than the fabric covering her. Still, she took his breath away.

When he'd heard the bids starting to escalate and saw the expression on Sam's face change from a smile to one of someone undergoing severe emotional turmoil, he knew he had to top them. He could not let any other man hold Sam in his arms and comfort her.

"I have one thousand," Marcia called over the microphone. "Do I hear more?"

A.J. held his breath waiting. Other than some scattered whispers, the room remained silent. Sam grew paler.

"Going once, twice…one dance with Samantha Ellis sold to the gentleman in the back for one thousand dollars. The children in the burn unit thank you, sir."

A.J. hurried toward Sam. Not until she stepped out of the spotlight and started down the stage stairs did A.J. realize she was in worse shape than he thought. Her complexion looked like death warmed over and her stride was shaky. He could see a fine sheen of moisture covering her face. He quickened his step.

"Sam?" He took her elbow. "Are you all right?"

"I will be in a minute," she gasped. "I just need fresh air."

A.J. guided her through a pair of French doors and onto a patio. The humid night air closed in around them. The heavy perfume of some flowering plant climbing all over the wall saturated the air. She dropped heavily into one of the chairs and gulped in several breaths.

Relief loosened his tight nerves when, thanks to a shaft of light from one of the ballroom windows falling across her face, he could see her color returning.

"Are you sick?" he asked, squatting in front of her. "Do you want to go home?"

She shook her head. "No. I just need to get my bearings. This isn't the first time I've suffered from stage fright."

Stage fright? That's what had her in this state? A.J.'s mouth fell open. He recalled their conversation at Rachel's about Sam's childhood. "You mean at all those beauty pageants, you—"

"Almost every time," she said, offering him an embarrassed, weak smile.

He sat beside her and held her hand. "Sam, this isn't stage fright. This is stage terror. How could your parents keep putting you through this?"

"Parent," she said, avoiding his eyes. "Just my mother."

"Why didn't your father do something to stop her?" If Sam had reacted similarly to the pageant circuit, A.J. was appalled that no one had stepped in.

A brittle laugh escaped Sam. "He didn't know. My mother said it was all in my head and that eventually I'd get over it." She laughed again, and this time the harsh sound squeezed his heart in a tight fist. "Guess I fooled her, huh?" She shrugged.

"Why didn't your dad know?"

Sam drew in a deep, shuddering breath. "It wasn't as bad when he was around. He walked out when I was ten."

"Walked out?" A.J. didn't think he could be more surprised at the events of Sam's childhood, but he'd been wrong. That any father could just walk away from a child made his blood boil. "You mean he just up and left?"

She nodded. A black curl broke loose from her upswept hairdo and fell against her neck. He fisted his hands to keep from touching it.

"I hated him for leaving us with her. He knew how strong and manipulative she was. They fought every night about me. He wanted to stop the pageants. She didn't. She told him he could leave if he didn't like it. I guess he took her words to heart."

Unable to stop himself or to find words that would erase the hurt from her heart, A.J. circled her shoulders with his arm and pulled her close to him. They sat that way for a long time, each lost in their own thoughts. Finally, Sam pulled free.

"I guess I'd better go find whoever it was that bought my dance and pay up." She stood and smoothed the wrinkles from her dress.

"Uh, that would be me." A.J. looked a bit embarrassed at having to admit he'd bid on her dance and hoped she wouldn't be mad because he had.

"You?" She knew she hadn't registered who had made the final bid, but she never suspected it would be A.J. Despite having done everything to avoid just such an eventuality, the idea of dancing with him suddenly seemed so right. Infinitely thankful that it wouldn't be some sweaty-palmed guy more interested in groping her than dancing, Sam held out her arms to him.

"Well then, let's do it."

When they stepped onto the dance floor and Sam heard the slow, dreamy music playing, her certainty about dancing with A.J. grew a bit shaky. Encircled by his arms while dancing to this kind of music could prove to be dangerous, very dangerous. But after she found herself enfolded gently in his embrace, her head resting against his shoulder and their entwined hands tucked between them, she knew that, for now anyway, there was nowhere she'd rather be.

"I see you've recovered."

Sam pulled back to see who'd spoken. Marcia Hilary

and the commissioner waltzed by them. She was rapidly learning to dislike Kevin's mother.

"Yes, I was just a bit dizzy," Sam called after them with a forced smile, then grimaced up at A.J.

Beside them Kevin moved awkwardly around the floor with a very pretty young woman Sam didn't recognize. Her heart ached for the young firefighter. She'd been fortunate enough to escape her mother's childhood tortures, but Kevin was still living with his.

"Poor kid," she said, her voice low so only A.J. could hear.

"Forget them." He pulled her closer.

Taking A.J. at his word, she did just that. Sam closed her eyes and rested her cheek against his wide chest. His heart beat strong and steady in her ear. They glided over the floor to the music, as if they were one person, totally in rhythm with each other's movements. Marcia, Kevin and all the other people surrounding them on the floor disappeared. Her world consisted of just A.J.

For tonight, she could allow that to happen. She was playing with fire, but for tonight she'd live her long-suppressed dream of A.J. being hers—and hers alone.

A.J. couldn't believe he had Sam in his arms, and that she wasn't trying to get away. He breathed in her intoxicating scent and nestled her even closer. He could feel the movements of her thighs against his, the soft brush of her hair on his face, the feel of her silky skin beneath his palm on her back.

If he died at this moment, it would be as a content man. He just wished it heralded a future filled with more nights like this one. But he'd only be fooling himself if he believed that. He and Sam had no future. If nothing else convinced him of that, he had only to look at his track record. The only future he had to look forward to was one with the BCI—fifteen hundred miles from the woman nestled in his arms. Just the thought brought a pain shooting through his chest.

When the time came, would he have the strength to walk away from her? He had no way of being sure he could.

For both their sakes, he had to.

The band finished one song and had just started another when Kevin appeared at their side. "May I steal Sam for this dance?" he asked A.J. very formally.

A.J. let Sam go. "Sure, if it's okay with Sam."

Nodding her agreement, Sam stepped into Kevin's arms. He held her awkwardly, with at least a foot of space separating their bodies. As they turned and moved about the floor, Sam noted that A.J. remained on the sidelines, his gaze fixed on them. A tiny thrill coursed over her.

By the time Kevin had stepped on her toes for the fourth time and spouted a profuse apology, all her concentration had centered on keeping her feet at a safe distance and praying for the dance to end. Kevin might have the potential to become a good fireman, but she had serious doubts about him ever making it on the dance floor.

The music was just winding down when Sam felt a tap on her shoulder. She turned to find Joe Santelli standing behind her.

"Something's come up at the firehouse. I have to leave. I've asked A.J. to drive you home." His hurried words sounded a bit frantic.

"Is it a fire? Should we come, too? Do you need help?" Kevin asked before she could say anything.

Santelli shook his head. "No fire. You guys stay and enjoy the rest of the evening. If I do need you, I'll call."

Before Sam could ask what the emergency was, Santelli had disappeared into the crowd. Seconds later, A.J. stood beside her, his face wreathed in concern.

"Any idea what that was all about?" she asked.

He shook his head. "Not a clue." Then he smiled. "Kevin, may I steal Sam back for the next dance?"

Kevin grinned. "Of course, sir. Thanks, Sam."

She thanked Kevin for the dance and then, without protest, slipped back into A.J.'s arms like a homing pigeon coming back to its nest. Being in his arms again had to be one of the most emotionally precarious positions in which she'd ever knowingly put herself. She'd worry about the repercussions tomorrow. For tonight, she'd let her heart take the lead. Snuggling closer to A.J.'s chest, she closed her eyes and allowed him to guide her around the floor.

For a few minutes, they danced in silence, A.J. once more basking in the glow of holding Sam. Her perfume and her soft skin beneath his hand acted like a strong aphrodisiac on his senses. His mind began to drift to places it should not venture, places like a dark room, silky sheets and sweaty entwined bodies bathed in silvery moonlight. A trickle of sweat rolled down his back, tickling the flesh between his shoulder blades.

A.J. stopped dancing and stepped back abruptly. "It's getting hot in here." In more ways than one, he told himself. "What do you say we get a drink and go out on the patio for some air?" He tried not to notice the disappointment on Sam's face. He'd rather have stayed here where he had an excuse to hold her, but if he did, they'd both end up regretting it.

"Sure. Okay."

With his hand on the small of her back, he guided her through the crowd and up to the bar. After getting a gin and tonic for her and an icy beer for himself, they headed to the patio and found a bench in a secluded corner.

Searching for safe ground for conversation, A.J. asked the first thing that came to mind. "So tell me, Sam, why would a former beauty queen become a firefighter?"

"Why not?" she replied, her lack of surprise telling him this was a question she'd heard many times before.

"Well, you have to admit that it's a strange transition and not something that happens every day."

Her gaze fixed on the horizon. For a long time she watched the waves kissing the beach in the moonlight. The muffled noise from the party going on inside filled the silence. He'd just about decided she was not going to answer him when she spoke.

"Lately, I've been asking myself the same question. I've even been wondering if I want to keep doing it. As a matter of fact, ever since I found that incendiary device in my house, I've been thinking about it a lot. I keep remembering when my mother died in that fire—" She stopped and shook her head as if trying to dislodge the memories. "I can't imagine dying like that."

A.J. wished he hadn't asked, hadn't revived the memories that obviously haunted her. He took her hands in his. "I'm sorry I asked. Let's talk about something else."

"The night my mother died…" she said, as if she hadn't heard him. She laughed without humor. "Maybe that's why I still go a little crazy when I know there's someone inside a burning building, and I can't get to them." She looked at him. "I bet a psychologist would have a ball with that, huh?"

"No, Sam, I think every firefighter feels like that."

Sam shook her head. "No, with them it's a need to save lives. With me, it's…" She sighed. "I sometimes wonder if I'm doing it for all the wrong reasons." She laughed again. "Boy, when I say it out loud, it sounds even flakier than it does when I just think it."

"Not at all." He wanted to help her, to explain why what she was feeling was natural, but he couldn't find the words. Instead, he pulled her into his arms. Besides, he felt as if she wasn't being totally honest with him. "What would you do if you gave up firefighting?"

"Work full-time with Rachel in FIST." The reply came so quickly, he knew it was something that she'd been considering for a while. "I really enjoy doing that work, but—"

"Sam. A.J. Thank God we found you."

Rachel and Luke stepped around the potted palm that provided an insubstantial barrier around them, but which had given them a modicum of privacy. The look on Rachel's face told them she wasn't about to impart anything good.

"What's wrong?"

Luke and Rachel exchanged worried glances before Luke spoke. "It's Joe Santelli. He's been in an accident."

Chapter 6

With Rachel and Luke right behind them, A.J. and Sam raced across the parking lot to his SUV. As she rounded the bumper and grabbed the door handle, a movement in the shadows caught her eye. Pausing for a moment, she concentrated on the shadowy figure.

"Get in," A.J. yelled, flinging open his door and climbing in.

Quickly, Sam roused herself and slipped into the front seat. A.J. put the car in gear and accelerated out of the parking space. The car lurched forward. As they careened out of the lot and into the flow of traffic, she swung around and stared out the back window. The figure she'd seen had left the protection of the shadow to watch their retreating car. In stunned disbelief, she realized it was the old man from the firehouse.

Who was he? What was he doing here? Was he following her? The possible answers made Sam feel as though a cold hand had gripped her soul.

Could he be the one trying to kill her?

It was the first time she'd actually assigned possible blame to a single individual, and the unanswered question tortured her thoughts as they tore through the late evening traffic. Finally, she shoved them to the side and concentrated on Joe and his well-being.

Rachel had told them that Joe had veered off the main highway running parallel to the Intracoastal Waterway and into a dry drainage ditch just north of town. No one seemed to know the extent of his injuries or if he even had any.

Sam tried to recall how much Joe'd had to drink, but she didn't remember seeing him with anything but club soda with a lemon wedge. He was on call at the firehouse, so he wouldn't have consumed any alcohol at all.

So, how had he gotten into an accident? He was a careful driver. Having ridden with him innumerable times before tonight, Sam knew he obeyed the rules of the road. He wasn't a candidate for road rage and tolerated the occasional stupidity of other drivers with amazing calm. But just because he drove within the law didn't mean everyone else on the road did. Maybe he'd been rushing to get to the firehouse and someone ran a stop sign or a red light. Maybe someone cut him off. Maybe...

How bad had the accident been? Suddenly, dread closed its icy hand around her heart. Images of Joe's maimed body trapped in his car accosted her. Tears blurred her vision. She gripped her shaking hands together and rung them until the skin felt raw. If she hadn't talked him into taking her, he wouldn't have been at the ball, and he wouldn't have had to rush back to the firehouse. If he hadn't had to rush back, he wouldn't have gotten into this accident.

"Damn!"

The expletive broke through Sam's thoughts. She jumped and glanced at A.J. It took a second to register what was happening. But then she noted A.J.'s white-knuckled death grip on the wheel, and his foot repeatedly pumping the brake pedal. Worst of all, it registered that despite his efforts, the SUV continued to hurtle forward at breakneck speed.

My God, the brakes aren't working!

Sam yanked her gaze from the driver and stared in horror out the windshield. The taillights of the car in front of them glowed red and they were closing in at an alarming speed.

A.J. spun the steering wheel to avoid a rear-end collision and bumped onto the road's uneven shoulder. He yanked on the emergency brake. The car went into a slide.

"Hold on," he yelled.

The tires caught the edge of the pavement and the vehicle jerked sideways. The seat belt biting into her shoulder and chest kept Sam from being thrown into A.J.'s lap. Face grim and lips set in a tight line, A.J. struggled to right the car.

Sam stared transfixed out the windshield. Looming right in the middle of their path stood a very large live oak tree. Her mouth opened in a silent scream. Terror had choked off her vocal cords. She dug her nails into the soft upholstery of the seat.

A.J. jerked the wheel the opposite way. Sam hit the side door hard. Pain shot up her arm. The seat belt cut deeper into her shoulder. Before she could react, the SUV thumped and bounced over the edge of the road, onto the median and into the southbound lane of traffic. Approaching car headlights blinded her. Tires squealed as oncoming motorists tried to avoid colliding with them.

A.J. spun the wheel again. Sam held her breath. The SUV squeezed between two of the southbound cars. Brakes screeched again. Quickly, he straightened the wheel and the car headed toward the only place left for them to go—the row of white guardrail posts bordering the waterway.

Sam gripped the dashboard and planted her feet on the floorboards. She wanted to close her eyes, but an insane need to see what would happen kept them open. A.J. managed to retain enough control of the direction of the car so that, rather than plowing over the bank into the Intracoastal Waterway, he used the guardrails to slow their momentum.

They sideswiped the guardrails for about twenty feet. The eerie screech of metal scraping across cement filled the air as the side of the SUV was torn open.

Their headlights bounced over the landscape and finally went out as the front fender was ripped free of the body. Glass shattered. Cars whizzed past them, zigzagging down the road in an effort to right themselves after veering to miss them. Finally, when she could stand no more, she closed her eyes and waited for the plunge into the Intracoastal. But it never came. She felt the car begin to slow and eventually lumber to a stop.

The night went deafeningly silent. Time crept by on dragging feet. Sam sat stone still, afraid if she moved she'd fall apart. A vague awareness of the pain of her nails biting into her palms seeped into her consciousness. She was alive. They were alive. Relief stole the stiffness from her tense body. She turned to look at A.J. He was staring fixedly out the windshield, his hands still retaining their white-knuckled grip on the steering wheel. Sam laid her head back against the headrest and waited for her heartbeat to slow.

"You okay?" he asked, his voice shaky.

Unable to speak, Sam nodded.

Feeling had just started to return to her extremities when, what seemed like hours later, Rachel and Luke, their faces white and drawn, peered into the windows.

"Are you two all right?" Luke yelled through the shattered window on the driver's side.

A.J. lifted his head from where he'd rested it against the steering wheel. Breathing erratically, he nodded. Blood had drained from his face and though he still hadn't released the steering wheel, his hands were shaking.

"Fine," he choked out. Then he turned to Sam. "You sure you're okay?"

Still unable to make her vocal cords work, she nodded.

"I called 911," Luke said, flipping the cell phone closed.

Rachel wrenched open Sam's door. "Come on. You need to get out of there."

Rousing from the grip of shock, A.J. grabbed his door handle, but the door was stuck, most likely a result of having sideswiped the guardrails. He slid across the seat to Sam.

"Are you sure you're okay?" he whispered urgently.

"Yes," she said, finally finding her voice. "My heart's racing and my hands are shaking, but otherwise everything seems to be working."

He took her hands in his, stilled them, then looked deep into her eyes. "I would never have let anything happen to you." He searched her face. "You know that, don't you?"

His declaration stunned her almost as much as the accident. "Yes." Her voice was weak and wispy and sounded far away. "I know." In her heart, she did. A.J. would always protect her. But who, in the end, would protect her from A.J.?

With blankets covering their shoulders, A.J. sat next to Sam on the back step of the EMT truck, the shock of their ordeal not quite having worn off. His knees were still too weak to support his body, so he didn't even try to stand. In his mind he kept replaying what had happened, why his brakes had failed.

Never in his life had he ever felt so helpless. To be speeding down the road at seventy miles per hour, hitting the brake pedal and finding out there were no brakes had been the worst feeling of his entire life. Even facing the muzzle of a gun hadn't been that bad. At least with the gun he had a chance of disarming the shooter. In the car he'd been looking death in the face with no power to stop it.

Sam stirred beside him. He turned to her. The many-colored lights of the emergency vehicles surrounding them washed her face, making it hard to gauge her state of composure. An overwhelming surge of thankfulness that she was okay infused his body, alleviating some of the coldness left by the trauma of the accident. He wasn't sure what he'd have done if anything had happened to Sam. Just the possibility left him awash in fear. To reassure himself that she actually was okay, he took her hand in his. She smiled weakly and tightened her cold fingers around his.

"You doing better?" he asked.

She nodded. "I was just wondering about Joe."

In the excitement, he'd forgotten why they'd been on the road to begin with. He sat up straight and searched for Luke in the crowd of people running around them. As if drawn by some silent psychic message, Luke made his way through the throng toward them.

"How's Joe?" Sam asked before Luke could say anything.

"He's fine. His car is totaled, and they still can't figure out how he got out without injuries, but he did, and he's okay."

"Thank God," Sam whispered and clutched A.J.'s hand tighter. "Where's Rachel?" she asked, looking over Luke's shoulder for her friend.

"I had one of my men take her home. I promised to call her as soon as I knew anything."

A.J. studied Luke's tense expression, half hearing their conversation. He knew his friend too well not to be able to see that something was bothering him. "There's more, isn't there?" Sam stiffened beside him.

For a second Luke looked heavenward. Then he centered his gaze on A.J. "Joe's brake lines were cut. They found out when they were putting the car on the wrecker's flatbed."

"Cut?" Sam stared from one man to the other. "But who would do such a thing?"

"From the description I got of Joe's car, I'd say you were really lucky, Sam, that you were with A.J. and not Joe...." Luke's voice faded into silence. He shifted his gaze to A.J.

The unasked question in Luke's eyes made A.J. go rigid. "My brakes failed, too." A pregnant silence hung between them. "Are you thinking what I'm thinking?" he asked Luke.

Luke glanced nervously at Sam, then nodded.

"Let's check it out." A.J. turned to Sam. "Stay here. I'll be right back."

She jumped to her feet and grabbed his hand. "No. I'm coming with you."

He almost said no, but then he saw something in Sam's eyes he'd never seen there before—fear. "Okay."

Retaining his grip on her cold hand, A.J. followed Luke past the police cruisers to the rear of the tow truck. The battered SUV sat atop the flatbed. The tow truck driver had just retrieved the fender from the middle of the road where it had landed after flying over the roof of the car. He threw it into the backseat of the SUV along with the rearview mirror and other debris from the accident.

A.J., Sam, and Luke circled the tow truck looking at the damage. He couldn't believe they'd walked away from this. Oddly, the right side of the car looked almost new. The left side, however, looked as if it had been through World War II. The crumpled hood was twisted grotesquely to one side. Deep, ugly gouges that looked as though someone had taken a can opener to it scarred the side door, and the shattered window's safety glass hung partly out of the frame. Both of the left-hand tires were flat, and the front tire had been torn partially from the bent rim.

Just looking at it made A.J.'s stomach flip. They'd been damned lucky to have gotten out alive.

Sam must have realized the same thing. "Oh, my God," she breathed, her gaze going from the twisted metal around the side door to him. "You could have been—"

His raised hand stopped her words. "I wasn't. I'm okay, and you're okay." When tears gathered in her eyes, he pulled her trembling body into his arms. "We're fine, Sam," he whispered against her hair. "We're fine." She nodded against his chest but continued to cling to him.

"You need to see this," Luke called from the side of the tow truck.

Keeping his hold on Sam, A.J. guided her to Luke's side. "What?" He thought he knew already and was proved right when Luke pointed to the cleanly cut end of a brake line.

"This was no accident, A.J., any more than Santelli's was. Aside from the cut brake lines and the failure of the air bags to inflate, there's one other commonality in all this and…" He glanced at Sam, then quickly looked away.

Sam felt a chill race up her spine. She hadn't thought about the air bags. "What?" She dropped A.J.'s hand for the first time in over an hour and stepped past him to stand in front of Luke. He avoided looking at her and instead stared at A.J. Grabbing the lapels of his tux, she shook him, wanting affirmation of what her common sense was already telling her. "What's the commonality, Luke?"

From behind, A.J.'s big hands gripped her shoulders. Luke looked at her for a very long moment. She knew what he was going to say before he said it, but she had to hear the words.

"You."

Even though she'd expected it, Luke's confirmation filled her with dread. Then just as suddenly, her fear turned to frustrated anger. Pulling from A.J.'s grip, she paced the small space around the tow truck, her mind racing for answers. Rage bubbled up inside her, heating the spots chilled by the accident. For the first time in the last hour or so, she felt alive, furious to the max, but really alive.

"Dammit! Who could be doing this? And why? I'm not a bad person. What did I do that would make someone want to kill me and hurt my friends in the process? Who—"

A flash of memory interrupted her tirade. She swung back to Luke. "There was a man…in the parking lot when we left tonight. It's the same guy who's been hanging around the firehouse. He was out there the day my car blew up."

"Do you know who he is?" Luke had his cell phone out and his finger poised over the keypad. "Can you give me a description?"

She shook her head. "I never saw him before. He's an older man. I don't think he's homeless. At least he doesn't dress like he is. He looks like any typical senior citizen. Maybe a little under six feet, average build, salt-and-pepper hair. He had on a blue sweatshirt tonight and dark pants." She grimaced. "Sorry I can't be more helpful."

Luke punched in some numbers. "I want a patrol car to check out the parking lot at the Palms. Send another one to check the area around the firehouse. You're looking for an old man...." He moved away from them as he repeated the description Sam had given him.

A.J.'s arm slipped around her shoulders. "They'll find him, Sam, and just maybe it will bring an end to this nightmare." He hugged her close, and she took comfort in his embrace. "In the meantime, I don't think you should go home until they find him. We'll go by your house, pick up whatever you need, then put you up in a motel—"

Sam tore herself from his arms and backed up, staring at him through wide, fear-filled eyes. "No! I'll sleep on the street before I go to a motel!"

Chapter 7

A.J. stared at Sam, unable to comprehend what had brought on her vehement refusal to go to a motel. "What is it? What's wrong?"

The fear in her eyes seemed to grow. He stepped toward her, his hands outstretched, but she backed away.

If she didn't want to go, he was not about to force her. "Sam, you don't have to go to a motel if you don't want to."

The fear remained in her eyes. She took another step away from him.

A.J. racked his brain for a way to reassure her. Then he got an idea. He'd probably regret this, but he couldn't stand seeing a woman who had shown such strength throughout this ordeal crumble before his eyes. "It's okay. You don't have to go to a motel. You can come home with me."

The fear drained from her expression instantly. To his surprise, she nodded her agreement.

"I'm sorry. I'm probably being foolish," she stammered, "but I just can't—"

A.J. enfolded her in his arms and held her tight. "It's okay. You don't have to do anything you don't want to do."

He had no idea what prompted her fear. All he knew was that he'd die trying to protect her from being hurt by anything or anyone. And if she was going to spend the night at his house, that included *him*.

The one word Sam could find to express her first impression of A.J.'s home was *cold*. The spacious condo boasted a spectacular ocean view, but the inside of the place was stark, impersonal, as if he were afraid to put his identity on it. In contrast to her house, which she'd filled to overflowing with herself so that it bore her indelible imprint, his home could have belonged to anyone.

No pictures or mementos, no family photos, no personal touches of any kind littered the walls or tabletops. The cold chrome, glass and leather furniture left her feeling unwelcome. The floors, devoid of carpeting or even throw rugs, added to the impression of a house filled with furniture for a strictly utilitarian purpose.

Sam sat on the sofa while A.J. made coffee in the stainless steel kitchen. Who was A. J. Branson? What made him live in these emotionally detached surroundings? What did she really know about him? Nothing, except he had the power to turn her emotions upside down with a mere touch or look.

The big question was, did she want to know more?

The answer was a resounding *no*. To know more would bring her closer to this man, something she couldn't and didn't want to risk.

"I'd like to freshen up," she called to A.J. "Where's the bathroom?"

"Down the hall and to your left."

Sam followed A.J.'s directions. Pushing away the questions about A.J. that haunted her, she hurried to the bathroom, washed her face and arms, then returned to the living room. A.J. was just setting a tray with two steaming coffee mugs, sugar and cream on the coffee table.

"I put your overnight bag in the guest room," he told her as he sat beside her and added cream to his coffee.

"Thanks." She fixed her coffee and took a tentative sip of the hot liquid. The aroma of freshly brewed coffee, normally a smell she loved, made her stomach churn. Must be nerves, she told herself. After all, they'd nearly died in a car accident.

Then again, the butterflies in her stomach might just be a result of being alone with a man who played on her emotions with all the vengeance of a Category Four hurricane hitting the Florida coastline.

The silence stretched out uncomfortably between them.

"Back on the patio at the hotel," A.J. finally said, "when I asked you why you became a firefighter, you talked all around the answer, but I got the feeling you never told me exactly why."

Sam cringed inwardly. If this was an attempt to distract her from the events of the past few hours, he'd sure picked a lousy subject.

For a moment, she remained silent, not sure if she wanted to share her gut reaction to one of the most traumatic events of her life, feelings she'd never shared with anyone. But then A.J. wasn't just anyone. He was the man who had sworn to protect her. If she couldn't trust him with the dark corners of her past, who could she trust? She took a deep breath and began talking.

"The night of the motel fire, when my sister Karen and I watched them carry my mother's charred body away on a stretcher, became a turning point for both of us. We realized for the first time in our lives that we had no one to account to except ourselves. We could do whatever we wanted. After the funeral, Karen left. I haven't seen her in a few years. I think she's working as a freelance photographer in New York."

Sam paused for a moment, suddenly aware of how much she missed her sibling and how much Karen hated her for the life they'd led. She couldn't blame her. Karen had been virtually invisible to their mother. Everything had revolved around Sam and the pageants. Karen's needs were never considered. Her camera had become her best friend and as time wore on, she'd spent more and more time with it.

"And you?" A.J. asked. "What did you do?"

"Nothing for a while. I just enjoyed not having to climb onto a stage, not having to feel my stomach tighten into sickening knots every night and parade myself in front of all those ogling people. Then that wasn't enough. I got to thinking about how my whole life had fallen apart around me, and how I had nothing to show for it except a few trophies, some certificates to hang on the wall and a broken family. I needed to do what Karen had done, put meaning to my life." She paused and drew in a deep, fortifying breath.

"My father had walked out. My mother was dead. My sister had faded from my life. Unlike Karen, I had no skills, no way to support myself, nowhere to go. I was trapped in a career as superficial as my foundation makeup. I couldn't believe how empty my life had become, and worst of all, how totally without purpose."

She glanced at A.J. He'd been so quiet she wasn't at all sure he'd been listening. With his gaze fixed on her, his eyes overflowed with concern. He smiled encouragingly.

"Then I thought about all those firemen racing into that burning motel room, despite the risk to themselves, to save a woman who had already given up on life. I was in awe. I so admired what they did. They saved lives and homes on a daily basis. They contributed to the community in a way I never had or could if I continued to be nothing more than a face and a figure."

She picked up her mug and sipped at the lukewarm coffee. Replacing it on the table, she continued.

"I finally decided I'd been robbed of my childhood, and I would not be robbed of one more moment of my life. I had just won the Miss Florida Pageant and was about to vie for the Miss America title, and I decided it wasn't enough. I wanted to do more with my life than decorate a runway in Atlantic City." She paused, realizing that with the telling of her story a huge weight had been lifted from her body. "That week, I walked away from the pageant, flew back to Florida, applied at the fire academy and never looked back."

A.J. remained silent as he stared down at the coffee mug cradled in his large hands. Then he turned sideways and faced her. "Is your mother's death in that fire the reason you didn't want to stay in a motel?"

A humorless laugh escaped her. It had taken A.J. a few moments to realize what it had taken her years to conclude. Sam stood and walked to the sliding glass doors that opened onto the balcony overlooking the ocean. Moonlight painted silver streaks across the undulating water.

"I haven't been in a motel since." She could feel him watching her.

A.J. studied her stiff back. For a proud woman like Sam to admit to what she'd just told him had to have scraped her emotions raw. Then he saw her shoulders slump and begin to tremble. She was crying, deep silent sobs. He wasn't sure when he moved, he just knew he had to be there to hold her. She burrowed her face against his chest. Her entire body shook as the sobs tore from her.

"I hated her. I was happy she was gone…but I… didn't want her to…die. I didn't." She drew back, and the sight of her tear-streaked face just about tore his heart from his chest. "If she hadn't been drinking… If Karen and I hadn't gone to that movie…" A new burst of sobbing erupted, and she melted against him.

A.J. led her back to the couch. He eased her down and then sat beside her, drawing her trembling body to his. At this moment, he would have gladly taken her pain on and weathered the agony rather than see her like this.

Lifting her chin with his forefinger, he looked deep into her eyes. "Honey, all the ifs in the world won't change what happened. But you have no reason to blame yourself. You were a kid, and your mother was an adult who knew what she was doing. Had you not gone out that night, you and Karen couldn't have stopped her from drinking, and you two might well have died in the fire, too."

As the explanation passed his lips, a bone-chilling thought followed on its heels. A world without Sam? For the very first time, he considered what that would mean, how desolate it would be, how totally intolerable. Never in his life could he recall feeling such despondency, such pain. His arms tightened around her.

Sam cuddled against him, absorbing his warmth and strength. As the sweet aroma of her perfume drifted up to him, his body sprang to life. He bit down hard on his lip and told himself this was nothing more than her delayed reaction to the trauma of the night's events, a need for something solid to cling to in a world that had tipped off its axis. After all, the woman had been stalked by a killer for days, and she'd nearly ended up in the Intracoastal or worse, dead. Her emotions were bound to erupt at some point, and he was just a convenient shoulder to lean on. It meant nothing.

But while his logical mind made excuses for her

actions, his heart kicked in and his need to carry her off to his bed and love her into the night intensified. Long-tamped yearnings pushed to the forefront of his mind.

He fought to block out how good her body felt pressed against him, how perfectly the planes of his fit with hers, and how much better it would feel skin to skin. The awareness grew stronger, threatening to push him into doing something they'd both hate themselves for in the light of day. He had to stop it before it went any further.

Gently, he pushed Sam away from him and held her at arm's length. "I think you should take a nice hot shower and get a good night's sleep. You'll feel much better about everything in the morning." He stood and stared down into her tearstained face and fought the urge to take her back into his arms with every ounce of strength in him.

Sam looked into A.J.'s startling blue eyes. She wanted many things right at that moment and none of them included a shower and a good night's sleep.

All of them included him.

She'd probably hate herself in the morning, but she'd take that chance. Right now, she wanted one thing—to be made love to by A. J. Branson. And for once, she would not deny herself.

Being held by him had made her feel safer and more secure than she ever had in her entire life, even in her beloved house. But was A.J. any different than Sloan had been? Would he eventually betray her and walk away like her father and sister had? Dare she risk her heart and trust him?

Then he smiled, and she knew the answer. Standing and leaning forward, she placed her lips lightly against his. His arms snaked around her, pulling her so hard against him that she could feel his shirt buttons branding her skin just as surely as his mouth branded her.

Why had she waited so long for this, fought so hard against it, when she'd wanted it so desperately?

But then, A.J.'s mouth grew more insistent and all thought vanished from her mind. Instead she focused fully on the texture of his lips and how he molded their mouths together as though nature had fashioned them specifically for this purpose. Her lips parted in silent invitation.

Her breath caught when she felt his tongue sweep the inside of her lower lip, then go on to taste more of her. Heat suffused her entire body. She strained to get closer to him, hating the clothes that kept them apart, if only by fractions of an inch.

Sam curled her arms around A.J.'s neck and allowed him to lower her backward onto the couch. The weight of his body pushed her deep into the soft leather cushions. He drew back and stared down at her. His forehead furrowed.

"You're hurt," he said softly. Then he leaned forward and gently kissed the spot on her shoulder where the seat belt had left a bruise. "Your skin is like warm silk," he murmured, brushing his lips across her neck and to the spot just above her exposed cleavage.

Her nails dug into his shoulders, urging him on, telling him that she needed him to touch her. Instead, it seemed to rouse him from his sexual stupor. He pulled back.

"This is not a good idea," he told her.

She blinked and sat up. His expression was as serious as death. Her first impulse was to hide, to take the humiliation of his rejection and run. Then she looked closer at him and saw the dark desire in his eyes.

"Aren't you as tired as I am of fighting this attraction between us?" she asked in a low, husky voice that sounded nothing like hers.

A.J. stared at Sam, trying to decide if admitting to what she suggested would be a good idea. If he said no, it would be a lie, and he'd be denying them both a night to be tucked away in their memories forever. If he said yes, he might well be opening a door for both of them that should remain closed. This wasn't the first time he'd faced a damned-if-you-do-and-damned-if-you-don't situation, but he'd never known one that would break his heart with either choice.

If he paid attention to his conscience, he would *chase* her off to bed. If he listened to his heart, he'd *carry* her off to bed.

His heart won out. "I am *very* tired of fighting the attraction."

She grinned, and his heart leaped into his chest and pounded out a hard rhythm.

"Then I suggest we do something about it."

Tension seeped from his body, to be replaced by a free yearning that took charge of both his mind and his heart. He laughed out loud, then scooped her into his arms and headed down the hall to the master bedroom.

Chapter 8

A.J. laid Sam on the bed, then sat beside her. Her dark hair, loosened from the confines of her upswept hairdo, splayed out in stark contrast over the snowy pillowcase. He hovered above her and stared into her beautiful face, unable to believe she was actually in his bed and with an invitation in her blue eyes that made his blood pump wildly through his veins.

He knew with a certainty that defied denial that he'd hate himself in the morning. Right now, if all the hounds of hell had been baying at his heels, he couldn't have stopped what was about to happen. Sam had offered herself up to quench his thirst and hers. For now, it was right. Later, it would have to be enough.

Carefully, he traced her full lips with the tip of his finger, then let it trail down her chin and over the creamy flesh bared by the plunging neckline of her gown. Her eyes closed. She sighed deeply and began to stir restlessly. Her back arched, begging him wordlessly to touch more of her.

When he didn't, she opened her eyes. Holding his heated gaze with her own smoldering one, she reached for the back of her neck to release the halter strap of her gown. A.J. stopped her.

"No. Let me."

Carefully, he released the gown's hooks, then very slowly peeled the top down her body. When moonlight bathed her naked breasts, A.J.'s breath caught in his throat. Her skin looked like that of a porcelain doll— creamy white, smooth and flawless except for one tiny mole on the side of her left breast.

He bent and kissed the mole, oddly pleased with the proof that Sam was not all perfection. She groaned and pushed her flesh against his lips. He smiled, then to answer her silent plea, moved his head and engulfed the turgid tip with his lips. Sam cupped his head in both hands, holding his mouth prisoner against her.

Waves of desire bathed his soul, washing away any lingering doubts about what they were about to do. He drew away. She clutched at him.

"I'm not going anywhere," he said softly, then gently kissed her.

Grabbing the material of her gown, he slid it over her hips and off her feet. Stunned into speechlessness by her beauty, he dropped the gown noiselessly to the floor. His gaze surveyed the woman before him. All she wore beneath the gown were thong panties so brief they hid no more than mere inches of her skin from his sight. But even that barrier was too much for A.J. He wanted to see all of her, every last inch.

Hooking his fingers in the waistband of the panties, a slim string spanning each hip, he quickly removed them. They joined the discarded gown on the floor. She lay naked before him, every inch of her body exposed to his starving gaze.

"My God, you are the most beautiful thing I have ever seen," he said, his voice breathy and hoarse with desire.

The compliment didn't seem to please her. Her gaze clouded. Instantly he realized what she was thinking. He sat beside her and gathered her close. She had become too used to people seeing her beautiful outer shell and not bothering to look beneath it.

He kissed her deeply, very gently and very thoroughly, then looked into her eyes. "Did you feel that?" She nodded. "That's your real beauty, Sam. That's who you really are. There's something inside you that reaches out to me. Something I can't define. Something inside you that you offer to everyone you meet. It's what makes you the person you are. Not this beautiful shell that all the world sees, but the beautiful soul that lives inside you."

Something broke free inside Sam. Something that had been caged up deep down inside all her life. And this man had seen it and let it free to grow. All her life she'd lived with empty compliments and insincere praise. All her life she'd had to be the person that everyone else expected her to be. With just a few heartfelt words, A.J. had given her the right to be herself for the first time in her life. He would never know the truly magnificent gift he had just given her.

The ribbon binding her heart in a neat, safe package fell away, allowing A.J. to inch into her soul. Gratitude so intense she could barely control it welled up inside her. She touched his face gently. "You're a pretty good guy yourself, Detective Branson." Then she kissed him as gently as he'd kissed her. "Thank you."

He smiled, and she felt her blood begin to heat again. She moved and his shirt front rubbed across her bare breasts.

"I think," she said, slipping the first stud on his dress shirt from the buttonhole, "that you have far too many clothes on, sir."

He caressed her cheek with the back of his fingers. "But aren't you about to remedy that?"

"Absolutely."

She slipped from the bed and drew him to his feet in front of her. When all the studs had been released, she slipped his shirt from his shoulders. It landed on her crumpled gown at their feet and was followed quickly by his T-shirt.

When her fingers dipped into the waistband of his trousers, A.J. sucked his breath in sharply. Sam smiled, glad that he'd dispensed with his formal attire's cummerbund earlier. The fewer barriers between them, the better. She was growing impatient with the layers of clothes separating them. Quickly, she divested him of his trousers, briefs and socks.

Finally, he stood naked before her. Sam drank in the

sight of him. Muscles rippled in his arms and chest. His tanned, flat stomach was marred only by a scar next to his navel. Daring not to let her gaze roam any lower, she raised it to meet his heated stare. She ran a fingertip lightly down his chest and stomach.

A.J.'s legs wobbled. His breath hissed through his clenched teeth. Groaning, he dragged her into his arms and captured her mouth in a soul-searing kiss. She snaked her naked leg around his hip and felt the heat of her femininity sear his hot skin. Together, they collapsed on the bed, their mouths still glued together.

His warm, strong hands traveled over her bare flesh, searching, learning, touching everywhere. She in turn touched him, exploring all the hills and valleys of his magnificent body. His skin felt like hot suede, smooth, firm and taut.

When his fingers dipped into her wet heat, she gasped and cried out. Sparks shot through her body. Longing such as she'd never known grew and grew until she thought she'd explode with the intensity of it. This play had gone on long enough. She wanted A.J. inside her and she could barely wait while he donned protection.

Sam rolled them so that she was on top of A.J. Slowly, her gaze never leaving his, she lowered herself on him. Sensations over which she had no control rushed through her. She collapsed on top of him.

With one deft movement, A.J. reversed their positions. He took control of their lovemaking and, too weak and too much in need to protest, she let him. His touch was driving her crazy.

Their bodies thrashed wildly, straining for completion. Then A.J. stiffened above her. His breathing ceased. His grasp on her hips tightened. Sam's body tensed. She sucked in her breath and waited for the world to turn upside down.

The rush of burning sensation built and built to a pinnacle. Her muscles strained and throbbed. Release came with a surge of sensation that rocked her to her very core. They clung together, letting the waves of passion wash over them, then ebb, leaving behind the placid sea of exhaustion.

Sam slept quietly beside A.J., her head resting on his shoulder, his arm tucked protectively around her. Her warm breath feathered his sweat-soaked skin. The regular rise and fall of her body told him she was at last free of the demons that haunted her during her waking hours.

While she was content, A.J. could feel the glow of their lovemaking giving way to regret.

What have I done? I added one more problem to her already overloaded list. Nice going, Branson.

What the hell had he been thinking? That taking her to bed, as mind-blowing as their lovemaking had been, would magically solve everything? That once his raging testosterone had been appeased he could walk away, leaving both of them untouched? That Sam would suddenly change her mind about wanting a relationship or that the emotional residue of his bad marriage and failed engagement would vanish like smoke in a light breeze?

He slid quietly from the bed, walked to the closet and pulled out a suitcase. Slowly, he began putting clothes

into it. Getting out of here as soon as possible, before
he hurt Sam, was the only answer. When he'd filled it,
he placed the suitcase back in his closet. He'd finish
later. When the time came for him to leave, he would
go fast and without any second thoughts.

He glanced back at the sleeping woman in his bed.
She'd thank him in the end.

Sam's eyes were barely open when the events of the
previous evening—the ball, the accident, the incredible
lovemaking with A.J.—came flooding back. She sat
up in bed, her screaming muscles reminding her even
more pointedly of the extent of the strain they'd been
exposed to the night before, both in the car accident and
in A.J.'s bed.

The accident was not something she cared to remember, but the night in A.J.'s bed brought a satisfied
smile to her lips. The man was amazing, just as she'd
always suspected he would be. The pitiful attempt at
lovemaking she'd experienced with Sloan Whitley
paled woefully by comparison.

With A.J., the satisfaction went beyond just physical.
He instinctively knew what a woman wanted and
wasn't afraid to give it to her. He shared himself and
all he was and touched her emotionally in ways she'd
never known before and in places in her heart that she'd
kept locked away for a very long time.

Sloan had never given more than he needed to make
himself happy. What she felt and how she felt had
mattered little, if at all, to him.

Sam pushed thoughts of her disastrous relationship

with Sloan out of her mind, stretched and found that, if she turned her head, she could smell A.J.'s aftershave on her shoulder. Smiling contentedly, she swung her feet to the floor, then padded to the closet to find a robe. Flinging the door open, she stared in surprise at many empty hangers and a packed suitcase on the floor of the closet. Absently, she wondered if A.J. was going somewhere.

As she hurried through her morning ablutions and left the bathroom, the aromas of bacon, coffee and either waffles or pancakes drifted to her. Her stomach growled. She quickly dressed in the jeans and bright yellow blouse they'd picked up at her house the night before and then hurried to the kitchen, looking forward to breakfast with A.J.

A.J., jeans and T-shirt molding his fit, muscular body, was busy flipping golden brown pancakes when she entered the room.

"Morning," she said, kissing him on the cheek and stealing a strip of crispy bacon.

"Morning," he mumbled, his concentration on removing the pancakes from the griddle and placing them in a neat stack on a plain, navy blue plate.

For a moment, Sam watched him. Was he trying to avoid looking at her? Was he regretting the wonderful night they'd just spent together? Was she just being paranoid?

Concluding she'd make a lousy behavioral analyst, she took a seat at the table and sipped at the glass of frosty orange juice, enjoying the caress of the cold, sweet liquid as it slipped down her dry throat. A.J.

placed two plates on the table and took a seat across from her.

He put his elbows on the table's edge, then steepled his fingers and spoke. "Luke called this morning. He said they picked up the old man you saw, but he's not giving them much."

Sam stopped in the middle of pouring syrup over the pancakes. "Can you talk to him?"

A.J. shrugged. "I could, but this is Luke's case and because of my…personal connection, it's better that he handle it so there's no hint of impropriety."

"Then let me talk to him."

He studied her for a moment, his face reflecting his disapproval of her suggestion, then he shook his head. "First of all, you're a civilian and have no official right to question a suspect for any reason. Second, the brass would go off the wall if we let you interrogate a suspect. They'd have my ass and Luke's. We don't want that, right?"

Sam felt a bit deflated, but she had no desire to get either Luke or A.J. in trouble. "No, I guess not. It was a crazy suggestion. Forget it." She would have liked to confront this jerk and find out firsthand why he was targeting her, but if it would impede them from learning anything, she'd wait. "I just thought, since it's me he's trying to kill—"

"He's *suspected* of trying to kill you. Remember, innocent until proven guilty? Until we have solid evidence that it's him, we can't assume anything."

"Okay, suspect. I just thought he might talk to me, maybe let something slip."

"Forget it, Sam. That only happens on TV. Let's just let Luke do his job. When I find out anything, I'll fill you in." Without another word, he dug into his breakfast.

While she swallowed bits of pancake that suddenly tasted like dry sponges, she stole glances at A.J. He concentrated on his food with much more intensity than simple eating required. She'd been right. A.J. was regretting their night together. An image of the packed suitcase drifted into her mind.

"So, where are you going?"

He glanced up at her, his fork halfway to his mouth, his brow furrowed. "To the station. I thought I just said that."

"I was referring to the packed suitcase in the bedroom." Biting into a strip of bacon, she chewed and studied his face.

"Oh, that. I…uh, just got back and haven't had time to unpack yet. I'll do it later today." He dug into the pancakes again.

All the happiness she'd felt from spending the night in his arms drained from Sam. She'd been around A.J. a lot lately and no one, not him, not Rachel, not Luke, had mentioned him taking a trip of any kind. A.J. was lying. Why?

Only one answer made any sense. A.J. was going to run off without telling her—just like her father had.

Though the day had barely begun, the OGPD buzzed with activity. The plastic chairs lining the wall were filled with shackled men and women who'd been arrested the night before and now awaited transportation to the courthouse for their bail hearings. Everyone from drunks to drug users to prostitutes eyed A.J. as he passed them on his way to his office at the back of the building.

As he'd driven the car the OGPD had loaned him to the station, he'd tried in vain to concentrate on what lay ahead in one of the interrogation rooms, but his thoughts kept veering back to the woman he'd left at the firehouse. Sam had looked so defeated, and he held himself responsible for that. If he'd been thinking with his head instead of another part of his anatomy the night before, he'd have shuttled her off to the guestroom bed—alone. But he hadn't done that. Instead he'd given in to the longing he'd seen in Sam's eyes, a longing promoted by nothing more than the trauma she'd experienced that night. She'd been as vulnerable as they come, and he'd pounced on her like a lion on its prey.

Well, he'd make sure it wouldn't happen again. Turning into his office, he went straight to the desk, flipped on his computer and, after it booted up, began typing.

Dear Major Clarkson;
In regard to your recent job offer with the New York State Bureau of Criminal Investigation, it's my pleasure to accept the position. Since I am required to give at least three weeks notice to the department, I should arrive in NY sometime after the end of the month.
Yours truly,
Austin J. Branson
Chief of Detectives, Orange Grove, Florida PD

He'd call the major a little later, he told himself, not analyzing why he wasn't eager to pick up the phone. He hit Print and waited while the printer spit out the document that would take him fifteen hundred miles from the people he loved. That last word exploded in his head with all the force of a bomb. *Love.*

My God, the one thing he hadn't wanted to happen had sneaked under his radar. He'd fallen in love with Sam. But that didn't change anything. He'd loved his ex-wife, too, and the woman he'd been engaged to when he'd run away from his pain to join the Detroit police force. Love hadn't stopped those relationships from blowing up in his face. The memory of that pain remained vividly imprinted on his mind, and he was not about to experience it again.

More important, he could not hurt Sam that way. She didn't want a relationship, and he would not do anything to change her mind. If she couldn't come to him freely, then…

His decision to leave seemed even more sensible now. Staying here and watching her, but never being able to have her, would be more than he could stand. Now that they had a very good suspect, it would seem that the solution was near and the attempts on Sam's life would soon end. That would free him to move on. He even had a packed suitcase ready and waiting.

The printer went silent. He removed the letter from the delivery. Reading it over one last time, he signed it, then pulled an envelope from his desk drawer.

"About time you showed your face," Luke announced from the doorway.

A.J. flipped the letter over. After Luke's last reaction

to his job offer, he didn't want him to know that he'd accepted and face another argument with him.

"Sorry. I had some stuff to take care of."

Luke grinned knowingly. "That *stuff* wouldn't happen to have long black hair and a figure to make a strong man weep, would it?"

A.J. ignored him and stood. "Let's get this interview with your suspect over with, shall we?"

Luke grabbed A.J.'s forearm. His grin had vanished and been replaced by a serious frown. "She's been hurt enough, A.J. Don't hurt her any more. If you aren't sincere about a relationship with Sam, walk away now."

"I don't need you to tell me how to run my personal life," he snapped.

"I'm not doing anything of the kind. I'm just giving you fair warning. If Sam gets hurt, you'll have a lot of people after your sorry butt. One of them will be me."

A.J. pulled his arm from Luke's grasp and stared him down. "I will do everything in my power to make very sure that Sam doesn't get hurt. Now, can we get on with this? That is if you can mind your own business for an hour or so."

Chapter 9

A.J. observed Luke and the old man from the fire-house through the one-way interrogation room window. Sam was right. He didn't look homeless. His short-sleeved summer shirt still had the sharp creases left by an iron and his spotless khaki pants showed no signs of wear. His lined face was clean shaven.

Just as he reached for the switch to open the speaker and listen in on the conversation, Luke stood, shook the man's hand, then left the room.

"Well...? Who is he?" he said to Luke, when the door had closed.

"His name's Tom Warren, and I'm turning him loose."

A.J. couldn't believe it. "Why?"

Regardless of what he'd told Sam at breakfast, just the fact that Warren was at the scene of at least two of the attempts on Sam's life made him a very viable suspect in A.J.'s eyes.

"Because he's not our man."

Anger and frustration rose up in A.J. He fought it down. He'd thought that this arrest would bring an end to the attempts on Sam and that she'd finally be able to resume her life. And that he'd be able to get on with his. He'd been so damn sure of it, he'd addressed the envelope and stamped it. Why he hadn't actually put the letter inside he carefully avoided thinking about. Now, Luke was telling him this Warren guy didn't do it.

"And you concluded this from what?" A.J. asked, his voice a bit more strident than he meant it to be.

"He had an alibi for the day Sam's house caught fire. We verified that he wasn't even in town." Luke leaned against the wall and sipped at a container of Latte Factory coffee, made a face, then threw it into a nearby trash can.

"What about the parking lot and the car blowing up? He was seen at both places."

"He says it's coincidence. He lives near there, and he walks that way every day for his heart. I saw the scar from his heart surgery, A.J. The bench happens to be the halfway point where he stops to rest."

Openmouthed, A.J. stared at Luke. Frustration threatened to choke him. "Are you telling me that a scar and a daily walk makes him innocent? Give me a break."

"No, it doesn't, but until I get more evidence to the contrary, it doesn't make him guilty, either. I have no reason to hold him." He ran his fingers through his hair.

"A.J., you've always trusted me before, let me handle this. I love Sam, too, and trust me, I won't let anything happen to her." He smiled wryly. "Rachel would kill me."

Luke's words took the fire out of A.J.'s anger. *I love Sam, too.* How had Luke guessed he loved Sam? Had he been so transparent?

He watched Luke walk away down the corridor. "You better not let anything happen to her, my friend," he said under his breath, "or you'll have more than an angry wife to contend with."

A.J. knew two things for sure. The next time he saw Tom Warren, he'd have a few questions of his own to ask him, and he better have more substantial answers than a bad heart and a daily walk. The other was that until they found out who was after Sam, he'd have to keep their relationship on a strictly business basis. He couldn't take a chance that there would be a repetition of last night.

After he mailed that letter, he'd have three weeks to tie up all the loose ends. But he hadn't mailed it, yet.

Did he really want to?

Sam hadn't been able to concentrate all morning. She'd started typing up the fire reports for the week several times and gotten no further than filling out the first one. She kept seeing that packed suitcase in A.J.'s bedroom. Where was he going? Why wouldn't he tell her? And how long was he going for? A week? A day? For good?

That same empty feeling she remembered coming over her the morning she woke up in a dingy motel room to find her father had walked out came over her.

Back then she'd felt so helpless, so abandoned. The thought of A.J. leaving left her feeling the same way and, if possible, even worse.

After last night, how could he leave? Didn't their lovemaking mean anything to him?

And exactly what did it mean to you, Sam?

Three weeks later, A.J.'s blood was at a full boil and had been ever since Luke told him what Santelli planned to do. He charged into Santelli's office unannounced.

"Have you lost your mind?"

From the resigned look on Santelli's face, A.J. knew Joe had been expecting him.

Santelli threw his pen on the desk, crossed his arms over his chest, glared at A.J. and leaned back. "I wondered how long it would take for Luke to tell you and for you to register your protest."

"Can the small talk, Joe. Why the hell are you putting Sam back on a truck?"

Santelli uncrossed his arms and rested them on the desktop. "I've got a job to do, and that job is none of your business."

Incensed, A.J. placed both palms on the desk and glared back. "If it concerns Sam's safety, it damned well is my business. How can you put her back on the truck?"

Santelli ran his fingers through his hair and stood. "Do you think I want to do this?" he yelled back, his features distorted in anger. Then he took a deep breath. When he spoke again, his voice had calmed considerably. "I don't have a choice. I have a community to protect, and I have four men out with food poisoning. That leaves me shorthanded. I need Sam on that truck."

Knowing his love for Sam fueled his unreasonable anger, A.J. fought to contain it. "You'll get her killed. You know that? Are you willing to accept that responsibility?" His voice had quieted, but his words were spat out from between clenched teeth.

With frustration showing clearly on his face, Joe slumped back in his chair. "There haven't been any attempts for almost three weeks, A.J."

"That doesn't mean this crazy son of a...that he's given up. He *will* try again, and having her on that truck will make it all too easy for him. She'll be a sitting duck."

"Look," Joe said, his hands splayed out before him, palms up, "if it makes you feel any better, I haven't told her yet, so I won't put her on the truck unless it's absolutely necessary. If we can handle the calls without her, I'll keep her here. But if I need her, A.J., she'll be on the truck just like all the other firefighters in this station house. Either way, it's my call."

Although it wasn't what he wanted to hear, A.J. knew that was all Joe was going to give him. If it had been the other way around, he'd have made the same decision. That didn't make it any easier to stomach. If he had his way, he'd wrap Sam in cotton and stow her in a deep, dark cave until this maniac was behind bars. However, he wouldn't have his way and even if he did, there was no way Sam would agree to hiding herself away.

Never in his life had he met a woman who could be

as stubborn as Sam or as courageous. Not once during this whole mess had she complained, with the exception of being taken off the truck and put on a desk. Even when she collapsed emotionally, it hadn't been because attempts were being made on her life.

A.J. nodded and left Santelli's office with a ball of fear and misgivings in his gut big enough to stop a bulldozer.

Sam entered the firehouse for her twenty-four-hour shift with a much lighter heart than she had in days. Since the night of the accident, there had been no more attempts on her life, and she'd even managed to fool herself into believing that it was over and that whoever had tried to kill her had finally given it up as a bad idea.

She'd bought a new car with a generous insurance check, attended Maggie Sutherland's birthday party, where she even managed to steer clear of A.J. for most of the day. There had been only one tense moment: when she found herself alone with A.J. while Rachel and Luke had taken Maggie and Jay to the park playground, and left them holding down the fort at the birthday picnic table. Someone had called A.J. away, and thankfully, there had been no need for her to make an excuse to leave.

It had been more than difficult sitting there, looking at him and being unable to touch him. But she'd weathered it and survived, just as she'd weather any more incidents that came along, until she got past this gnawing attraction to the man.

Sam stowed her purse in her locker and had just stepped into the apparatus bay on her way to the duty desk. She hadn't even made it past the truck when the alarm went off. The strident sound filled the apparatus bay, echoing and reechoing off the walls. The firehouse came to life around her like a hive of disturbed bees. Men ran in all directions gathering equipment, donning turnout gear and hopping on the respective trucks.

This was the first call they'd gotten since four of their guys had come down with food poisoning. She stepped to the side to get out of the way of the firemen hurrying past her to the trucks.

Santelli came running from his office. His soot-covered helmet sat askew atop his head, his left arm was in the sleeve of his bunker coat and his loud voice echoed around the apparatus bay, yelling orders to the men. As he slipped his right arm into the other jacket sleeve, he headed straight toward Sam.

"Get your buns on the truck, Ellis. It's a big one."

"What?" Sam stared, openmouthed.

"On the truck. Now!"

"Yes, sir." She started forward.

Santelli grabbed her arm. "Just watch your ass, okay? I don't want to have to explain to your boyfriend why we brought you home in a body bag." His grim expression told her that he was not happy about reinstating her to active duty.

Her heart thudded excitedly in her chest. Before he could change his mind, she bolted for the truck, grabbed her turnout gear and jumped onboard.

* * *

The chief hadn't been kidding about the size of the fire. By the time the pumper truck on which Sam rode arrived, the east wing of the old hotel on Ocean Boulevard was well on its way to being one of the biggest fires they'd fought all year.

While the west side of the building seemed virtually untouched by the fire, the deafening roar of the snaking fingers of orange flame curling from the east side of the building promised to spread very quickly. Heat radiated from the inferno that made one of Florida's hot summers seem like springtime in the Rockies. The stench of burning building materials clogged the ocean air.

As the first company on scene, Santelli took charge as the incident commander. He began hurling orders out to the men. He turned to her. "Ellis, you and Hilary go into the west end of the building and check to make sure no homeless people have been using this as a rest stop."

Disappointment at being put in a section of the building that would prevent her from being in the thick of the action slipped into her mind. She pushed it away and concentrated on the job Joe had given her and Kevin. Though she knew that the sick feeling would come afterward, the adrenaline pumping through her body right now heightened her excitement about being back in the job for which she'd been trained.

Sam jumped down from her perch on the truck and slipped on her Nomex hood, carefully tucking it inside her turnout jacket, and placing the regulator hose and connection outside of the hood. She adjusted the hood so that her vision was not blocked, but enough that it still protected her neck and head. After donning her gloves, she checked to make sure she had all her equipment, grabbed a pickax from the side of the truck and headed toward the burning building.

As she moved, she glanced up at the structure ahead of her. She could see the glow of fire that threatened to spread to the west wing. The hotel had been deserted and condemned for years. It was the perfect place for the homeless to take refuge, but carelessness on the part of one of them could be the reason it was now engulfed in flames. Nevertheless, they had to make sure no one was inside.

"Move it, Hilary," she called to Kevin.

Just as she approached the smoke-filled doorway, she caught sight of A.J.'s car pulling up in front of the building. She paused long enough to see him step from the car, then search the throng until his gaze settled on her. In her heart, she knew he had no way of telling who was inside the turnout gear, but she liked to think it had been his heart that had guided his gaze to her.

She took a deep breath. "Let's go," she said to Kevin, and stepped into the wall of smoke blocking their path.

Chapter 10

Straining his eyes to see through the haze of stinking smoke, A.J. searched for any sign of Sam. Then his gaze fell on two firefighters going into the west end of the burning building. They stopped and one of them turned back and looked in his direction. As though an invisible thread stretched between them, he knew instantly it was Sam. For that moment, she seemed to stare directly at him, then she turned and vanished behind a wall of thick black smoke.

A few windows away, he could see the orange glow of the approaching fire reflecting off the interior walls. The growl of the angry flames devouring everything in their path filled the night. He'd been to enough fire scenes to know that it wouldn't take long before the blaze ate its way to where Sam had gone into the building.

His heart rose up to choke off his breathing. His fingers curled into tight fists. His entire body throbbed with the need to follow her, to pull her out. The impossibility of both instincts bowed his shoulders under the weight of his anguish. At that moment, he understood how Sam had felt the night she stood outside the motel fire that killed her mother. He couldn't stop Sam, and he had too much respect for her to even try. That didn't mean he didn't want to with every breath of life in him.

A.J. had never felt so totally helpless in his life because, until Sam emerged safely, he could only wait and pray. Waiting wasn't his strong suit, and praying would be an exercise in futility. God had stopped listening to him a long time ago.

Sam and Kevin had reached the top floor and, although there was no sign of flames, just thick, blinding smoke, they could hear the roar of the approaching blaze. As Sam passed one of the rooms, she thought she heard a voice calling out for help. She stopped dead and listened. It came again. Faint, but she heard it.

When she looked up to alert Kevin, he'd vanished into the wall of impenetrable smoke. Uncertain whether to pursue him and bring him back, she hesitated. The cry came again. Behind her the roar of the fire grew closer. Going after Kevin could mean the difference between life and death for whoever it was.

Taking off her glove, she tested the temperature of the door. The wood was comparatively cool. She put her glove back on, then entered the room. The oddly shaped room was narrow and long, with one high, small window and a crumbing wooden floor. Smoke poured into it through an air duct above her head. Pausing, she listened, but heard nothing, just the incessant approach of the fire.

Then, noticing what appeared to be a closet door at the far end, she headed toward it. Hiding in a closet was not unusual in a fire. The door to the room slammed shut behind her, probably from the wind created by the heat.

The smoke had become quite dense at an alarming rate and even with the help of her flashlight, Sam was having trouble finding the closet door she'd been able to see just moments ago. Whoever was in here, she had to get them out soon. She ran her gloved hand down the wall horizontally. When it came in contact with the doorknob, she tested the wood for heat, then, finding it cool, quickly twisted the knob and threw open the door.

The closet was empty. She turned to retreat. An impenetrable wall of black smoke blocked her path.

Since Sam had entered the building, time had ticked by in slow motion. Unable to stand and watch any longer, A.J. searched the crowd of faces for the fire chief. Finally locating him near one of the pumper trucks, A.J. hurried to him and grabbed Santelli's arm. "Why isn't she out of there, yet?" He had to scream to be heard over the din of the fire.

"She's checking the upstairs rooms for people. It takes time," Joe said impatiently over his shoulder as he hurried away to supervise the direction of a hose being used to wet down the west wing of the hotel.

A.J. ran his fingers through his hair, never taking his gaze off the burning building and the west wing door. "Come on, Sam. Get out of there. Come on." He whispered the plea to himself, hoping against hope that his words would penetrate the smoke and find her.

"What's happening?"

A.J. turned to find Luke and Rachel standing close beside him. Luke's arm was slung protectively around Rachel's shoulders. He still hadn't gotten used to her not getting upset at a fire.

"Sam's inside," A.J. said, his voice shaking almost as much as his hands.

"I thought she was off the truck until we found—" Rachel's elbow to his ribs cut Luke off.

"Joe put her back on the truck out of necessity. He was shorthanded."

Luke's large hand settled on A.J.'s shoulder. "She'll be okay. She's a tough lady."

Nodding, but saying nothing, A.J.'s gaze went back to the west wing. The reflection of the flames eating their way across the building had gotten closer to Sam's location.

Suddenly, a thunderous roar rose above the cacophony of the fire. He turned to see the east wing collapse in a shower of bright sparks and curling flames. His heart followed it down. How long before the west wing did the same thing?

I will not die without a fight.

The black, impenetrable fog imprisoning Sam wrapped around her like a shroud of death. The deafening roar of the fire reminded her of the thunder that accompanied a tropical storm.

Air. Check air pressure.

Lungs straining, Sam felt for the metal indicator hooked to the shoulder strap of the air cylinder backpack, then tilted it toward her face. Shining her flashlight through the haze of smoke, she read the bad news…less than quarter full. A quick check of her backup gauge verified it.

Damn! Why hadn't the alarm gone off to let her know her air supply was running low?

A sinking sensation filled her stomach.

Looking around, Sam aimed her flashlight at the opaque wall of smoke. The beam hit it and reflected back at her. Totally disoriented, she swung around, searching for an escape route. The gray smoke surrounding her grew steadily thicker. Anxiety threatened to close off her throat. Her breathing grew more rapid.

She fumbled for her radio. Her gloves made activating the talk button difficult. The clip holding the radio on her collar snapped. The radio slipped through her fingers, then clattered to the floor and scooted out of sight. Dropping to her belly, she pressed herself as low as she could manage while encumbered by the bulky turnout gear, and felt blindly for the radio. But she found nothing but wooden floor.

With shaky fingers, she fumbled at her waist, then tripped the manual switch on her personal alert device. She waited for the PAD's pulsating, high-pitched alarm to shriek out her location. Nothing happened. She smacked the device, hoping to activate it, but still it remained silent. Quickly, she removed a glove, then pried the cover off the battery case to check the contacts. The battery was missing. How in hell—

Damn! Damn! Damn!

She didn't have time to worry about the *hows* and *whys* now. Having exhausted every emergency device she had, she used the only thing she had left—her voice. Ripping the mask from her face, she screamed her partner's name over and over as loud as she could, hoping to be heard over the deafening rumble of the fire. Smoke was sucked down her throat, sending her into a coughing spasm. Still she continued to call out.

"Kevin! Kevin!"

Holding her breath, Sam listened for his response or the sound of his footsteps. Nothing. She yelled again, this time louder.

"Kevin! Kevin!"

The renewed roar of the fire beast ate her words and the smoke she was sucking into her lungs seared her throat and started another coughing fit. She was on her own, a prisoner in a world of smoke and flames that could mean agonizing death.

If only she hadn't come in here to investigate what she could have sworn had been a voice calling for help. If only she'd called to Kevin to follow her in. If only—

Opening her mouth to call out again, she decided against it. It would only waste more of her precious air supply and make her inhale more of the blistering smoke and heat. She refastened the mask over her mouth. Chances are, no one could hear her over the fire, anyway. She was alone, reliant on her own skills. She'd always been independent, wanted to be able to survive without anyone's help, but this total and complete isolation was not what she'd had in mind.

Clammy fingers of panic began to squeeze her mind. The veins in her temples throbbed. She'd never consciously thought about her own mortality before. Now, face-to-face with it, she didn't have much choice.

A lot of good all those trophies did her now. Would they find her charred body among the ruins? Trying not to think about how solitary her life had become in the past few years, she fought back the urge to cry out again.

Before her dwindling air supply sent her completely beyond the borders of sane thinking, she tried to organize her thoughts.

Panic kills. Stay calm. Think.

She squinted into the impenetrable wall of stinking black smoke surrounding her. On the other side of the wall she could hear the roar of the approaching flames eating away at the top floor of the abandoned building, getting steadily closer to where she was.

Move your buns, Ellis.

Panic gnawed its way to the surface again, trying to block coherent thought. She pushed back the rising fear.

Dammit, think!

She glanced at the pressure gauge. The needle rested closer to zero. As if on cue, her chest tightened.

Hard to breathe. Find door.

Crawling blindly, she stayed close to the wall.

Slowly, fighting to remain calm, she slid her gloved hand along the baseboard. Where the hell was the door? Her hand came in contact with what felt like a door frame. Carefully she moved it up and over the top, following the door's outline until she had found the knob. She turned it. It wouldn't move. Frantically, she rattled it, trying with all her strength to turn it, but to no avail. It was locked.

How did it get locked and from the outside?

Now was not the time to solve puzzles. She had to get out. Swinging the flashlight's beam from side to side, she hoped that it would penetrate the smoke and fall on something to give her a way out. Nothing. Nothing but gray-black death.

She pushed herself to her feet, head down, legs bent at the knees. Her head grew light. She stumbled. Flinging out her arms to counterbalance herself, she staggered to the side and slid down the wall.

Acutely aware of her quickly diminishing air supply, she started skip-breathing.

Inhale. Hold. Inhale. Hold. Exhale.

She should be doing something, but what? Thinking rationally was getting more difficult. Words tumbled through her head like water over a precipice. She tried to snatch at them, to find the ones that would save her.

Inhale. Hold. Inhale. Hold. Exhale.

Using her flashlight's beam, she glanced at the air pressure gauge on her strap.

Zero.

Straining to hear over the deafening roar of the approaching fire, she listened for the sounds of the other firefighters below. Once more, she dropped to her belly and pressed her cheek into the slivered, rotting wood. The stink of hot, acrid smoke seared her nasal passages and her lungs burned as if the fire had crawled down her throat.

Then the welcome sound of water pounding against the broken ceiling below her filled her ears. The good news was the other firefighters were wetting down the ceiling below her to prevent a burn-through. The bad news was that procedure would encapsulate the fire in the upper floor where she was.

Sam tore off the mask and pushed her face closer to the floorboards. Removing her remaining glove, she ran her fingertips over the gaps between the floorboards. When she found a wide crack, she slid toward it, then shoved her nose into the opening and breathed deep. Stagnant air trapped between the lower ceiling and the floor mixed with the putrid odor of burning wood and drifted up to fill her starving lungs.

Using her flashlight, she stuck it through the hole and then hammered as hard as she could at the ceiling below until she felt it give and the rush of heavenly oxygen hit her face. A fine mist of water found its way to her and sprayed her hot cheeks.

Moments later, she heard the sound of raised voices screaming her name. She thought one voice might be Kevin's. Then came a deafening splinter of wood and three figures burst through the wall of smoke.

Chapter 11

Sitting on the rear platform of the ambulance, Sam held an oxygen mask to her face. Periodically, she removed the mask to cough up black soot. Behind her, the collapsed ruins of the hotel's east wing and partially burned west wing served as a vivid reminder of how close she'd just come to death.

While she waited for her breathing to return to normal and her lungs and nose to stop stinging, her brush with death weighed heavily on her mind. This had been the closest she'd ever come to being another name on Engine Company 108's Memorial Wall, and the effect on her was nothing short of profound. Like most humans, she was of the it-couldn't-happen-to-me school of thought. That it *could* happen to her came not so much as a shock as it did as a very rude awakening.

Leaving the company to join Rachel in FIST was looking better and better all the time.

Her mind filled with all the things she'd never done: swimming with the dolphins, walking the beach at sunrise with someone she loved, going to Disney World. And the thought of the people she'd never told how important they were to her—her sister Karen, her friend Rachel Sutherland...

Most important of all, she'd never told A.J. she loved him. She did, with every fiber of her body. When she looked back on it, she couldn't understand why she hadn't recognized what had been happening to her all along. All the signs had been there for her to read: sleepless nights, erotic dreams, her response to him, the intensity of their lovemaking.

But there's still that packed suitcase, Sam.

"You okay?"

Sam jumped and looked up to find A.J. standing over her. Deep lines of concern creased his pale face, urgency filling his voice.

She forced a weak smile to her cracked lips. "Yeah. I'll—" she coughed "—live."

Though her hoarsely spoken words sounded careless, she felt the declaration all the way to her toes. She *would* live.

Profoundly grateful for her life, she looked around her. The organized chaos of firefighting went on without interruption, as though her life had not hung in the balance just minutes ago. Despite business as usual, she knew every man out there was worried about her— and wondered when it would be him sitting here thanking the powers-that-be that he'd escaped the fiery claws of death yet again.

But mostly, the fact that someone was trying their best to kill her seemed to sink in in a way that it hadn't before. And she wasn't the only one affected by that. As she stared up at the man beside her, she could see the stark fear etched in A.J.'s expression.

A.J. took a seat next to Sam. He had to hold her, to make sure she was actually there, alive and breathing. "Well, that you'll live is something." The blasé words hid the indescribable relief he felt right down to his toes.

He couldn't take his eyes off her. Soot and all, she was still the most beautiful woman he'd even known. Love swelled up in him like a stormy sea. It was all he could do to keep from telling her of his newfound feelings. But he was sure it was the very last thing she wanted to hear right now…or ever, at least from him. While he wanted to assume the role of the lover and more, instead he assumed the guise of the concerned friend.

He cleared his throat of emotion. "Have the EMTs checked you over yet?"

She shook her head. "Not yet."

He had an overwhelming need to get her away from here, away from the threat that still lurked somewhere out there in the darkness. He was remembering how close Rachel Sutherland had come to dying in a fire set by a maniacal arsonist a little over a year ago. For the first time, he really knew what Luke had gone through. How he'd needed to touch Rachel, to protect her, to make sure she was okay.

His grip on her hands tightened. Sam winced, and he loosened his hold. He could kick himself for not fighting Santelli on letting her go back on the rig. He should have insisted she be kept out of harm's way. He shook his head. Why was he beating Santelli up for something he'd had no control over? Santelli hadn't asked for the outbreak of food poisoning that had cut down his man power. Santelli hadn't set the fire to get Sam in the path of danger. It was all just a lousy coincidence.

Or was it?

He thought about something Sam had said over and over during their investigation of the arsonist that had kidnapped Maggie.

It's too much of a coincidence to be a coincidence.

He turned and scanned the crowd of onlookers and firemen for Luke. He caught sight of him standing a few feet away.

"I'll be right back," he told Sam.

Giving her hand a reassuring squeeze, he strode to Luke's side. "Did anyone check to see what caused that sudden outbreak of food poisoning at Engine one-oh-eight?"

Luke shook his head. "No reason to."

"Well, you have one now. I want to know why so many people came down with it."

Luke looked surprised and puzzled. "I don't—"

"Just do it," A.J. barked. "I have a feeling that the outbreak of food poisoning that put Sam back on the truck and this fire all happening within a day of each other are not coincidental. Take my car to the hospital for me. I'll be there with Sam." He threw Luke his keys and hurried back to Sam.

Forced to wait for the EMTs to check Sam out, he had to ask about one other thing that had passed the realm of coincidence, something that had been gnawing at his mind since Joe had told him they'd lost contact with Sam inside the building.

He squatted in front of her, took her hands in his and looked her in the eye. "I know you guys have emergency equipment for times like this. Why in hell didn't you use yours, Sam?"

Seeing no way around it, since the truth would come out soon enough, she sighed.

"Not…working," she finally choked out.

A.J. gasped. If possible, more blood drained from his face. "None of it?"

Sam took a large gulp of oxygen and avoided his eyes. She knew the conclusions he'd draw, and she couldn't disagree with him. That all her emergency equipment had failed at once was more than happenstance. Her stalker was back and, this time, he'd gotten inside the firehouse and come closer to killing her than ever before.

She shook her head. Before she could say more, another wracking cough tore through her aching chest. Her throat felt as if someone had poured acid down it.

A.J dug into an ice chest resting on the ground near them. "Here," he said, handing her a sweating bottle of ice-cold water.

She ran the bottle over her hot forehead, then removed the cap and drank long and thirstily, ignoring the resulting pain clawing at her throat and chest. The icy water felt like sweet life running down her painful throat. And right now, she had an insatiable need for anything life-affirming.

After drinking her fill, she pushed a long piece of her wet, smoke-saturated hair from in front of her eyes, then rasped out, "Thanks."

He gave a curt nod. Fear still filled his eyes, but his expression was one of the detective digging for clues. "What in hell happened in there? Why wasn't your equipment working?" His low voice held a distinctly controlled edge.

Sam peered up at him. He really seemed to care what happened to her. A rush of warmth invaded her body. Oh, she knew the chief and her fellow firefighters cared. Rachel cared. But knowing A.J. cared made a difference. She wasn't sure why, but it did.

Having been around A.J. for the last year, she was pretty much able to read his moods, but this was one she'd never seen before, at least not directed at her. She'd seen it with Rachel's kids, Maggie and his namesake, Jay, but this time even his tone was different. As though her safety meant more to him than just concern for another human being. The idea sent her heart thumping wildly against her chest. Was there a chance...?

To cover her discomfort at this new side of A.J., Sam took a long swig of water, then glanced up at him and opened her mouth to speak, but he stopped her with a raised hand.

"Never mind. Save your voice. We'll talk later."

Suddenly a thought hit her. She hadn't seen her probie partner since she'd gotten trapped in that room, and she was worried about his well-being.

"Kevin?"

"He's fine."

She exhaled a painful sigh of relief.

Before A.J. could say any more, an EMT stepped between them and took Sam's arm. "Sorry, Branson, we gotta get her to the E.R. and check her lungs."

"I'm coming with you." A.J. looked at her as if he expected an argument.

Sam grabbed his hand and experienced the same rush of security and comfort she'd had when she'd lain in his arms after they'd made love.

"If you didn't, I wouldn't go."

A.J. glanced at his watch. 12:22. Sam had been inside the X-ray room for over an hour. The few people who had been in the hospital waiting room had long since gone home, leaving him alone with his troubled thoughts. The only sound in the hall was the click of a computer's keys coming from the nurses' station.

He gulped the last of his cold coffee, then made a hook shot with the empty cup in the general direction of a gray metal trash basket. When it dropped neatly in, he shook his head in surprise. However, his preoccupation with the successful shot was short-lived.

His thoughts inevitably returned to the dilemma he'd been trying to sort out ever since he'd given Luke his orders to check out the food poisoning incident. Was it a coincidence that it happened the day before the hotel fire? Was Sam's failed equipment connected to it in any way?

Maybe he was grasping at straws, but it helped keep

his mind off the fact that Sam had almost died. Every time he allowed that to seep into his mind, his whole body went cold and the pain that shot through his heart nearly made him double over.

If he hadn't figured anything else out tonight, he knew one thing for certain. He would not be able to leave Sam. A gut feeling told him that if he left, he would lose any chance he'd ever have at finding happiness. And A.J. had learned long ago that a smart cop goes with his gut.

As soon as he got back to the office, he'd destroy the letter of acceptance he'd written to the BCI and draft a new one in which he'd turn down the job. At least he hadn't called to accept. Come what may, he was here to stay.

But by staying would he be sentencing himself to remaining at arm's length from the thing he wanted most in the world? Then he recalled Sam's response to their lovemaking. He knew she'd felt something for him, and he was damned well going to find out what it was.

Sam couldn't stop thinking about the fire and her narrow escape. By the time she'd been released from the hospital and settled on the leather couch in A.J.'s condo, she couldn't hold back the one question that had been beating at her brain.

"What do you think happened to my equipment, A.J.?"

He sat beside her and took her hand. "I think you need to forget about it for tonight, take a long hot bath, and then get a good night's sleep."

"But—"

He stood and pulled her to her feet. "No buts about it."

"A.J., you're mothering me." Her protest lacked conviction.

Kissing her lightly on the lips, he grinned at her. "Humor me, at least until I get used to you being alive and safe." He tugged her after him and headed down the hall to the master bedroom. "You get undressed. Here's a bathrobe. I'll draw a bath for you."

Before she could protest, he'd handed her his white terry robe, stepped into the bathroom and then closed the connecting door. Lacking the energy to protest, she took off her smoky clothes and slipped on the robe. She'd just secured the sash when a soft knock sounded on the bathroom door.

"You decent?"

"Yes."

The door swung open and the pungent smell of soap wafted to her. Over A.J.'s shoulder she could see the tub piled half-full with white suds. He took her hand and guided her into the bathroom.

"I'll be right in here if you need me," he said gently, then disappeared into the bedroom.

Being cherished was a foreign sensation for Sam. Never in all her life had anyone cared that much about her or her feelings or even wanted to take care of her. As odd as it seemed coming from this muscular cop, she found she liked it. She liked it so much that she didn't want it to end, especially not now, not when she'd come so near to death. For a long, indecisive moment Sam stared at the closed door.

She fisted her hands to keep from wrenching the door open and begging him to come back because she didn't want to be alone. Solitude wasn't something she needed right now. She'd had more than her share while trapped in that burning room.

You're being foolish, Sam. You just need someone, anyone, close because you're experiencing leftover trauma from a night of horrors. Besides, have you forgotten the suitcase? A.J. may be here tonight, but what about tomorrow and all the tomorrows after that?

She took off the robe and slipped into the warm bathwater. The bath level rose to just below her breasts. The foamy, fragrant water caressed her tired body, draining it of the tension of the last few hours. Clearing her mind of all troubling thoughts, she laid back against the tub, closed her eyes and allowed the comfort of her surroundings to overtake her.

A.J. sat on the edge of the bed, his face buried in his palms. Try as he might, he could not remove the images of Sam being carried out of that fire, of the stark terror of thinking she was dead. He'd never felt such utter and complete sorrow and loss in his life, as if his reason for living had suddenly been snatched away.

Then she looked at him and flashed that smile he knew so well. At that moment, life had poured back into his soul with such force that he'd almost cried out. If, before that instant, he'd had any lingering doubts about accepting that job and leaving here, they had all vanished like smoke on a stiff breeze.

He lifted his head and stared at the closed door. He

listened for the movement of the water as she bathed, but heard nothing. His body stiffened. Was she okay?

Without thinking, he got up, crossed the floor and opened the door. His breath caught in his throat.

Sam had slid down and rested her head on the edge of the tub, her eyes closed, her dark hair vivid against the white porcelain. His gaze rested on the slight rise and fall of her moisture-coated breasts. Each time she took a breath the rosy centers peeked at him, then disappeared beneath the surface of white bubbles.

Totally beyond his control, his groin tightened. Desire rose up in his throat. His active imagination drew pictures in his mind of what else lay hidden beneath the soapy bubbles. Pain shot through his hand, alerting him that he had been clutching the doorknob in a death grip.

Somewhere in the far reaches of his mind, he told himself to back up, close the door and leave her in peace, but he couldn't seem to either move his body or divert his gaze.

Good grief, Branson. There's an unpleasant name for someone who indulges in this kind of behavior.

With more effort than it should have required to do the honorable thing, he closed his eyes and turned to leave.

"Don't go."

Frozen in midstep, A.J. waited, afraid to breathe. Had he only imagined her voice telling him to stay?

"Please."

Reluctantly, he swung back toward her. Her open eyes were trained on him. Invitation glowed in their blue depths. Very slowly, she rose from the tub. Water and bubbles cascaded down her body in tiny, glistening rivulets. Little by little, the bubbles slipped away, leaving her entire body exposed to his heated gaze. The heat of the recent bath left a rich, creamy pink glow on her skin.

His blood rushed through his veins at breakneck speed.

She stood there, allowing him to look his fill, and said nothing.

When he could stand no more, he took a deep steadying breath. "This is very dangerous, Sam."

She continued to hold his gaze. "I know."

"If I stay—"

"I know," she said, her voice so low he had to strain to hear it. "I know exactly what will happen, A.J."

Chapter 12

A chill shivered over Sam. She wasn't sure if the cool air on her hot, moist skin, or the sensual thoughts racing through her mind, or the caress of A.J.'s gaze on her was the cause of it. When A.J. came to her with a fluffy yellow bathsheet, her mind stopped working entirely.

Carefully, as if one wrong move would shatter her, he enfolded her in the huge towel, then lifted her from the water and carried her into the bedroom. The unmistakable feeling of being cherished struck her again. She curled her arms around his broad shoulders and snuggled her face in the crook of his neck.

Giving in to a sudden urge of reckless daring, she tasted his earlobe, sucking it between her lips and bathing it with the tip of her tongue. When a deep groan issued from him and his step faltered, she smiled.

"Unless you want me to drop you, you better stop that," he said, but his deep voice quivered with husky desire.

"I'll take my chances," she murmured into his ear and repeated the tantalizing play.

His breath caught, then escaped on a long sigh. "This means payback, you know."

"I'm counting on it," she purred.

He turned his head so that their mouths were no more than a whisper apart. "You, my dear, are a seductive witch," he said against her lips.

Delighted with the sexual banter, she threw back her head and laughed. "That's better than some names I've been called."

Laying her on the bed, he hovered above her, his blue eyes darkened by desire. "Like what?"

She opened her mouth to speak.

He stopped her with a finger to her lips. "Like intelligent, compassionate, fiercely loyal, brave…loving?"

Sam's heart swelled. Over the years she'd been referred to as many things and looked at like a piece of meat put on display for the world to judge, but never had she heard any of these words applied to her.

Looking deep into his eyes and seeing only sincerity, she cupped his face in her hands. Happiness welled up inside her and filled her throat, so her voice emerged on a shaky note. "You have no idea how much that means to me."

Pulling him down to her, she placed her mouth gently against his. Without saying the words, Sam attempted to tell A.J. how much she loved him. The kiss was sweet, grateful and ultimately revealing of the feelings that lay within her heart for this man.

Though it began as gentle and tender, the kiss soon escalated to hungry and passionate. Removing her hands from his face, Sam encircled his shoulders and pressed their bodies together. She could feel his reaction pressing into her belly and ground herself against it.

Imprisoning her within his arms, A.J. rolled to his back.

He stared up at her. He knew Sam resided in his heart, but until this moment, he'd never realized that she made it beat, made his soul come to life, and gave him a reason to look forward to the sunrise. Without him realizing it, she had become an indispensable part—the very best part—of him.

Sam sat up and the towel dropped away, revealing her and all her naked beauty to his hungry gaze. With the tip of his finger, he traced a line from her chin to the cleft between her breasts, then he wrote his name in the moisture clinging to her skin.

"Mine," he said softly, then turned out the light.

Velvet darkness closed around them. No moonlight shafted through the window to illuminate the room, and they were forced to rely on the sense of touch to find and explore each other.

It took her only moments to find the buttons on his shirt. Minutes later, she had divested him of his clothes and they lay naked to the night, skin to skin. The heat from her body invaded his, warming all the cold places in his heart left behind by unfulfilled dreams.

"Sam." Her name slid off his lips like silk. He loved the way it sounded, as if that one word spelled out tomorrow and all the tomorrows to come.

She moaned deep in her throat and bit playfully at his neck and ears. A shudder coursed over him. Despite the heat of the night, delightful chills chased up and down his spine. He pulled her closer. This was his woman. This was his Sam. He ran his hands down her back, over her behind and back again, relishing her intense reaction to his touch.

Sam couldn't lay still. A.J. was driving her crazy. She strained against him, wanting more. At the same time, she wanted to prolong this night, to devour it like a starving woman, to store it away in her memory forever. She made him wait while she retrieved a small foil packet from the night table, ripped it open and put it on him.

He rolled her to her side. His hand slid between them and slipped downward, seeking out that spot where their bodies would eventually join and become one. When he found it, she cried out her pleasure. A gnawing, aching need began to grow inside her. Her mouth went dry and her fingers dug into his shoulders.

No one had ever affected her like A.J. No one had bothered to delve beneath her surface appearance and discover who she really, truly was. He'd seen her as a woman and found her soul. He seemed to understand what made her the person she was. And even knowing all this, he'd never tried to change one aspect of what he'd found.

Her thoughts came to an abrupt halt as he trailed

kisses over her shoulders, breasts, stomach and thighs. Her breath ceased. Her body arched. When she could take no more, she pushed him to his back and straddled him.

"My turn," she whispered against his chest.

A.J. waited. His breath caught in his throat. Then her feather-light touch was caressing his skin. She seared a path over his chest and down his stomach. He swelled and throbbed. Clenching his jaw, he fought for control. When she started lower, he grabbed her shoulders and pulled her back up until their faces were level.

"You best stop or this is going to end before it begins."

A girlish giggle issued from her, then she slid up him and positioned her body above him. Slowly, she lowered herself on him. He groaned and grasped her hips, helping her to establish a rhythm that would bring them both pleasure but not end this rapture too soon.

Throwing her head back, Sam let A.J. set the pace. Sensations far beyond simple explanation spiraled through her. Her skin felt supersensitive to his touch. Every movement of his hips brought her closer and closer to that indefinable ending. Her muscles tightened, preparing for the finale.

Suddenly, a rush of sensation flowed through her like floodwaters breeching a dam. She squeezed her eyes closed and held her breath. Lights exploded behind her eyelids, brighter than any fire she'd ever seen. It burned white-hot and fierce, then slowly faded to glowing embers.

Sam collapsed across A.J.'s chest. He looped his

arms around her and cuddled her close to him. As he did so, it occurred to him that he never wanted to let her go.

The next morning, Sam awoke and stretched like a contented cat. Memories of the night before clung to her mind like persistent cobwebs. The words A.J. had used to describe her drifted through her thoughts: intelligent, compassionate, fiercely loyal, brave, loving. A renewal of the glow they had created the evening before rushed over her. That he saw her as more than a pretty face meant more to her than any gift A.J. could have given her.

She lay there staring at the ceiling, remembering the touch of his hands, the warmth of his lips, the gentleness of his touch. Even their lovemaking, though just as intense as the first time, had been slower, easier, a thing to be savored. He'd handled her like a treasured porcelain doll and satisfied her like the wanton she became in his arms.

Sighing, she turned to the other side of the bed. It was empty. For a moment, she could have sworn her heart stopped beating, then she heard the sound of A.J. making breakfast. She slipped from the bed, donned his terry robe, then padded barefoot into the kitchen.

A.J.'s attention was on the omelet he had just slid onto one of the plates on the table. The table looked as if it had been set for a party. Stemmed crystal glasses filled with chilled orange juice sat beside each plate. Candlesticks flanked a bowl filled with flowers that rested in the center of the table. Linen napkins lay neatly folded beneath gleaming silverware.

Quietly, she eased up behind him and encircled his waist with her arms. "Good morning."

He turned toward her, hauled her to him and kissed her with an intensity that made her knees go weak. "Good morning. Ready for breakfast?"

"This looks more like a feast," she said, eyeing the beautifully set table. "Are those little red specks shrimp?" She pointed at the tiny specks of color scattered through the lemon-yellow eggs.

He kissed her again briefly, then guided her to a chair. "It's a celebration, and no, those are not shrimp. I'm deathly allergic to shellfish. It's red pepper."

"Celebration? Of what?" Sam picked up the glass of orange juice.

"You. Me. Us."

Without drinking, she set the glass down. "Is there an us?"

For a long moment—too long—A.J. stared at her. "You tell me."

Sam couldn't answer. She wanted there to be an *us*. She wanted it with everything inside of her. But, even after last night, she was afraid to believe, afraid to surrender that last small piece of herself that would leave her defenseless and vulnerable. Then there was still that packed suitcase in his closet.

He slipped his hand over hers. "Let's take it slow, okay?"

Relief flooded through her. She smiled and nodded, amazed that he could read her heart so accurately.

Her stomach growled, breaking the tense silence,

and they both laughed. Then the toaster popped up four slices of golden-brown bread.

"I'll get that," Sam said.

A.J. leaned his elbows on the table, watched her go into the kitchen and pull the bread from the toaster. As she buttered the toast, he studied her. Images of the woman in the bathtub drifted through his thoughts only to be replaced by images of the woman he'd held in his arms and loved into the night. He compared them to this woman in his kitchen.

She was one and the same, yet she wasn't. The woman he'd made love to was sure of herself, confident in her ability to satisfy him. The woman in the kitchen exhibited none of that assurance. Sam didn't have to say it for A.J. to see that emotional commitment scared the hell out of her.

Oddly enough, for a man who had felt exactly as she did less than a week ago, after last night his attitude had done a complete about-face. He wanted Sam, not just in his bed, but in his life and not just for today. He wanted to grow old with her. Never before had he been able to see beyond the moment with other women. But with Sam, he had a vivid picture of them sitting together on their fiftieth wedding anniversary and looking at each other with a love that had matured over the years into a bond that couldn't be broken by anything.

He sighed and waited while she placed a plate with buttered toast on the table, then sat again. If being patient with her now meant that down the line he'd be waking up beside her and then looking across the breakfast table at her each morning for the rest of his life, then patient he'd be.

"I talked to Luke earlier," he said, looking for a way to ease the tension that had suddenly filled the breakfast nook.

Sam's head snapped up. "And?"

"He wants us to meet him at the station. The ruins of the fire should have cooled enough for it to be inspected. He thought you'd like to be there while Rachel does the arson investigation. Since there's a chance that the fire was set deliberately as an attempt on your life, your role would have to be unofficial, of course. You up to it?"

She hesitated for only a moment, then nodded. "If it helps find out who's messing with my life, I'll be there." She looked back at her plate, moved a piece of omelet around, then raised her gaze to his. "You'll be with me, right?"

Vulnerability shone from the depths of her blue eyes. He took her hand in his and squeezed it reassuringly. "As long as you want me."

It didn't take A.J., Sam, Rachel and Luke long to find the point of origin for the fire. The arsonist hadn't been very clever. The stench of gasoline and the black V on a wall in the east wing, which indicated the point of origin, proclaimed it as loudly as if the arsonist still stood there, match in hand. Satisfied with the findings, Luke and Rachel had gone back to the police station to have the evidence Rachel had gathered processed.

"You ready?" A.J. asked, taking her arm and starting to guide her toward his car.

Sam stopped. "No. I want to go inside to that room. I want to know why I couldn't get out."

"Do you think that's wise?"

She turned to look directly into his eyes. "Yes. I *need* to see it for myself." Deep inside, she knew if she didn't go back there, going into another fire would be almost impossible. She *had* to get past this one.

For a moment he seemed to be giving her request consideration. She could read the hesitation in his expression.

"If you don't go with me, I'll go alone."

He nodded, then kissed her quickly. "Okay. Let's go."

She handed him a pair of disposable gloves and, as they slipped them on, they trooped across the grounds toward the hotel's west wing.

A few feet from the building, Sam stopped and pointed at one of the hotel's second-story windows. "That's the room I was trapped in. If this is a deliberate fire, then the arsonist forgot one crucial thing. The front of the building is missing some siding, and when Hurricane Edwina passed close to here a few weeks ago, the strong winds and torrential rain drenched the exposed wood and the humid air off the ocean kept it from drying out completely. It smoldered rather than burned. That produced a lot of smoke, but it probably helped save my life."

As always, when A.J. thought of Sam trapped in that room and not coming out alive, his stomach turned and a sharp pain shot through his heart. Both sensations served as a vivid reminder of how close he'd come to almost losing Sam forever.

A.J. dropped his gaze to the lower part of the wall and noticed something strange. He walked forward, then examined a line of melted plastic on the siding. Inside the plastic was wire. Above him another piece of the same material had melted into the siding. Still farther up and leading inside the window was more of the same wire.

"No wonder they went bankrupt. Their electrical work leaves a lot to be desired," he said, studying the piece that had fallen off into his hand.

Sam started to take it from him, but stopped and handed him her evidence case. "You better do this." He took the case. "If the arsonist hadn't burned the place down, this would have done the job eventually." She watched him turn the wire over in his fingers, examining it more closely. "That's lamp wire. Why would they have lamp cord strung on the outside of the building?"

Without giving her an answer, he dropped the piece of wire into a plastic bag he'd pulled from her evidence case, tucked it back in the case, snapped it closed and then picked it up. "Let's see what's inside."

A.J. stepped aside and let Sam take the lead.

Inside, Sam carefully climbed the stairs leading to the second floor room in which she'd almost died. The first thing she noted when she stepped into the room were several large brown stains on the wall, hot spots where the fire had started eating through the Sheetrock. When she thought about how close the fire had come to consuming the room and her along with it, she shivered.

Pushing such thoughts from her mind, she slowly walked the perimeter of the room. The door was partially charred where flames had licked at it, and the room itself stunk of smoke and dirty water. Partially burned wallpaper hung haphazardly from the walls in long strips. The flooring was warped from either time, water or heat, or perhaps a combination of all three.

In the far wall, about eye level, a large, square hole gaped. On the floor below it lay a metal grate, rusted and missing part of its frame.

"What's that?" A.J. asked, coming to stand beside her.

"The covering for that air duct." She pointed at the hole in the wall that was big enough to accommodate a small man.

When he didn't respond, she turned toward him. A.J. was dividing his attention between the duct and the glassless window near it.

"What?" she asked.

He held up a hand for silence, then walked to the window and leaned out. "Son of a—"

"What?" She waited for him to answer. When he didn't reply, she raised her voice a notch. "Dammit, A.J., what do you see?"

While she watched him in growing frustration, A.J. pulled himself back inside, then went to the duct. He drew a flashlight from his back pocket, switched it on and then shined it into the duct hole. Stretching so that his head and shoulders disappeared inside the hole, he extracted an old-fashioned, rectangular tape recorder. A device she didn't recognize protruded from the side of the recorder. A wire, a perfect match to the lamp wire they'd found on the outside of the building, dangled from the device.

"If the tape in this thing is still intact, I'll bet my next paycheck that it contains the voices you heard coming from this room." He held out the recorder for her to see.

While Sam was relieved that she hadn't been going nuts, she was still confused. "I don't understand."

A.J. fingered the device connected to the side of the recorder. "This is a remote control. It's the kind people use to turn on Christmas lights without having to go outside. It can be triggered to go on at any given time with the use of a small control that looks like the remote you use to operate your TV. It was simply a case of waiting until you were positioned and then clicking the recorder on so you'd hear the voice and go into the room."

"But how would this person know when I was outside this room? The place was full of smoke." She clicked open the case and removed a can that looked much like an empty gallon paint can. Holding it out, she waited until A.J. took it from her, slipped the recorder into the can, then replaced the lid and set it beside the evidence case.

For a time A.J. said nothing. "Sam, they had to be close to you. Who was with you outside the room when you heard the voices?"

A cold clammy chill swept over her. The only people who had been close by were fellow firefighters.

Chapter 13

A.J. guided Sam into his office. "You wait here, and I'll go find Luke."

"I'll come with you."

For a scant moment she thought he might let her go with him, then he shook his head and removed the metal canister containing the tape recorder from her evidence case. "You know you can't be connected with the chain of evidence, Sam. That's why I gathered everything at the hotel. You know that any defense lawyer will blow it apart in a courtroom if you touch one piece of this evidence." He ran his fingers lightly over her cheek. "When we finally catch this creep, I don't want any shadows hanging over the case. I want you to walk away without ever having to look over your shoulder again."

Disappointment swamped her. She so wanted to be involved in finding this jerk, but she also knew A.J. was right. If she was connected in any way with transferring the evidence to Luke, a judge could very well throw it out, and they needed all their guns firing properly to make sure whoever it was paid for what they'd done to her.

"Wait here. Okay?"

Waiting was not one of her personal strong points. Her father had always said if someone could rearrange time and make tomorrow happen yesterday, she'd have been a much happier child. But this was one time she didn't have a choice. As the old saying went, the wheels of justice turn slowly.

"You're right, of course." She forced a smile. "I'll stay here."

"Good. I'll be back in a few minutes."

A moment later, the door clicked shut behind him. At that precise moment, the nerves she'd been holding in check since they found the tape recorder made themselves known. Her hands began to tremble and sweat beaded her forehead. What if they didn't find this jerk? Would she spend the rest of her life, as A.J. had said, looking over her shoulder? Worst of all, she'd managed to live on her luck three times, but would the day come when she would not escape the attempts on her life?

Okay, Sam. That's enough. You're getting gruesome. Find something to occupy your mind until A.J. gets back.

She flopped down in the desk chair and looked around her. This was the first time she'd ever been in the OGPD chief of detectives' inner sanctum.

A.J.'s office was the exact opposite of his pristine, impersonal condo. In contrast to the mostly naked walls of his condo, framed commendations for his service to the OGPD and diplomas from various police training programs nearly obliterated the wall above the filing cabinets. In the corner a hat rack held a suit jacket and a navy tie with swirls of gold, red and green all over it. Both showed a light coating of dust. Obviously, neither had been moved in some time.

As she gazed around her, Sam realized that this office was A.J. as much as her house was her. This was where he lived and worked, where he felt confident, comfortable and secure. Where he felt safe, emotionally and physically.

Sam looked at the desk. Strewn across its surface were papers, file folders and writing instruments of all kinds, along with coffee cups with leftover coffee fermenting in the bottom. A couple had some unidentifiable gray stuff floating on top. Unable to believe this was the same man whose home was so clean it looked unoccupied, she glanced into one of the cups, curled her nose and gathered the cups together, sliding one inside the other. Then she threw the stack into the trash can beside the desk.

As she did so, she was struck again with how little she knew about this man who had stolen her heart. Rather than think about that, she busied herself straightening the papers on the desk into piles. The papers consisted of everything from completed reports to some he hadn't even started yet. To prevent mixing them, she began sorting.

She'd gotten about halfway through the pile when she noted one addressed to the New York State Bureau of Criminal Investigation. Feeling as if she were prying, she put it aside. As she did so, she noticed the words *it's my pleasure to accept the position.*

Sam felt as if a cold hand squeezed her heart. Instead of putting the letter aside, as she'd intended and knew in her gut that she should, she started reading from the top of the sheet. The more she read the harder that invisible hand squeezed her heart. When she'd finished reading it, she dropped it on the desk and stared at it, as if she could erase the words eating away at her soul.

Waves of intense and varied emotions battered her. First came pain so excruciating it felt as if someone had carved a hole in her heart with a dull, serrated knife.

A.J. was leaving, and he hadn't even told her. Instead he'd allowed her to think they had a future. The sound of her heart breaking and her world crumbling around her drowned out the noise of business as usual going on outside the door.

Next came anger. White-hot, soul-searing anger. Now she understood the packed suitcase in his bedroom, why she'd never told him she loved him, why she couldn't completely trust him with her heart, no matter how secure he made her body feel. Her subconscious had been warning her, and she hadn't been listening. Her stomach clenched.

The pain of his betrayal was almost more than she could stand. He'd let her believe he cared about her, let her fall in love with him, knowing he would never be able to return her love, or that he never planned on staying in Orange Grove. He'd betrayed her just like her father had, just like Sloan Whitley had, just like her mother had.

Finally a welcome numbness invaded her body. She continued to stare at the letter, still not wanting to believe what she was reading, then she put it on the desk, stood and quietly left the office.

A.J. and Luke exited the forensics lab and walked back down the hall toward A.J.'s office. "Hopefully, this won't take too long."

Luke scratched his head. "Well, you know that it depends on their backed-up cases, but I asked the lab to expedite it. If he does, then we could have some results later today. Tomorrow morning at the latest." He stopped at the opening of another hall leading off to the left. "I want to see if they have anything on the print we lifted from the recorder. I'll call you later when I know something."

Before Luke could move away, A.J. grabbed his hand and shook it. "Thanks. I owe you one."

Luke slapped him on the shoulder. "No, you don't. I told you before, we love her, too." Then he smiled knowingly.

A.J. saw no reason to deny what had to be clearly evident in his expression. "Yeah. I know you do."

For a while, he allowed his gaze to follow Luke down the hall, wondering if he'd ever find the kind of happiness his friend had. Would the day ever come when he'd go home to a loving wife and a beautiful child? Would there ever be a time when he'd know the peace and contentment of loving and being loved in return?

With a prayer on his lips that he wouldn't have to wait long to find out, he made his way through the reception area and then to his office. His footsteps echoed down the oddly quiet hall. After checking his watch, he knew why. The shift had changed, and this was the lull that always followed when the men on duty had gone out into the streets and those going off their shift were in the locker rooms changing into street clothes.

Eager to see Sam, he quickened his step until he stood outside the door emblazoned with his name and rank. Erasing any sign of worry from his expression, he opened the door. The office was empty. He glanced around and noted that someone had straightened his desk. Sam?

One paper laying haphazardly atop the pile, and that showed signs of being crumpled, caught his eye. He picked it up. The letter he'd written to the BCI. The letter he'd forgotten to destroy. The letter that Sam must have seen.

"Sam? Sam, are you in there? You can't hide. I see your car. Please, let me in so we can talk."

Sam could hear A.J. calling to her from her front porch, but she remained curled up in the fetal position on her bed. Didn't he know that there was nothing to talk about? He'd lied to her, and was going to walk out of her life. What more was there to say? More excuses? More lies?

"Sam? Please."

She grabbed the pillow and covered her ears until all she could hear was the sound of her heart breaking over and over. If she never had to look at him again, it would be too soon.

She'd thought the pain of finding out that Sloan Whitley was married was the worst betrayal she had ever encountered next to her father's desertion. But this far exceeded it. The love she'd felt for Sloan, she came to understand later, was that of a young girl flattered by the attentions of an older man. Loving Sloan had been a whirlwind of emotions she'd never experienced before, and had come at a time when, having just lost her family, she needed to know that someone loved her. As a result, she'd talked herself into loving a man that she not only didn't love, but didn't respect, either.

With A.J., it was different. She knew what love was and knew how deeply she'd felt it. She knew that, had he asked, she'd have spent her life loving him.

But he hadn't asked. Nor, it seemed, had he ever planned to ask.

With that admission, the pain came again, deep and searing. She drew her knees up to her chest and let the tears cascade down her face.

A long time later, the tears had dried up and the pounding on the front door had ceased. Outside, clouds covered the sun and a slow steady rain splattered her bedroom windows.

For over an hour, A.J. sat outside Sam's house, hoping she'd... What? Come running out to chase after him?

Face it, he told himself, *you screwed up again.*

From the very first he'd been afraid of this very

thing happening. He knew that relationships fell apart around him, but he'd ignored the inevitable and had hurt Sam as a result. He was beginning to wonder if he had a self-destruct button inside him that he used to deliberately sabotage relationships before he could get too close to a woman.

Maybe that could be true of other relationships, but not this one. He'd truly wanted this one to work. Also, unlike the other times when his job had come between him and the woman he loved, this time, it had been his own stupidity that had screwed things up. He should have destroyed that letter right away. Then Sam never would have seen it, and he wouldn't be sitting outside her house feeling as if someone had just ripped his heart from his chest.

But all the could-haves and should-haves weren't going to change anything. Somehow, he had to find a way to explain this to her, to regain her trust.

He laid his forehead against the steering wheel. His temples throbbed unmercifully. His heart ached endlessly. Finally, when no sign of life came from the house, he reluctantly put the car in gear and drove away.

The next evening, after the men had returned from a small brushfire in the north of town, Sam had just finished filling one of the air tanks and putting it back on the truck before she left for the day when she saw A.J. striding across the apparatus bay. Quickly, she slipped around to the opposite side of the truck, hoping he hadn't seen her.

"Sam."

Damn!

She kept walking, but could hear his footsteps on the cement floor right behind her. His hand closing over her upper arm stopped her retreat. He turned her to face him.

"Sam, we need to talk."

"About what, A.J.? About the way you lied to me? About your plans to move to NY? About the real reason for that packed suitcase? Exactly what is it you want to talk about, because I think everything is perfectly clear. Therefore, I think we've done all the talking necessary."

She pulled her arm free, and spun away. Several of the firefighters nearby watched as she hurried toward the locker room, A.J. following closely on her heels.

"You have to let me explain the letter. It's not what you think."

His tone dug into her heart, but she steeled herself against it. Stopping short and without turning, she challenged, "I don't have to *let* you do anything. As for explaining, if you'd been open and honest with me, there would be no need for explanations of any kind." Then she spun to face him. "And how do I know that your so-called explanation would not be just more lies piled on the lies you've already told me?" She turned away again, unable to look at him without crying. She'd shed enough tears for this man, or any man. "The letter was self-explanatory. Now, my shift is done, and I'm going home, so please excuse me." Her anger was spent, leaving her voice dead and devoid of feeling.

She continued down the hall and through the door

into the locker room. The lack of sound behind her told her A.J. wasn't following her. He had finally given up.

But as the locker room door closed, she thought she heard him say, "I never lied to you."

She closed her mind to him and anything he could say. When she reached her locker, she rested her forehead against the cold metal. In all honesty, she wasn't entirely sure whether his lack of effort to pursue her pleased her, or if she was disappointed that he hadn't tried harder.

By the time Sam got home, the mental exhaustion of the last few days had taken their toll. Her feet were dragging, and she couldn't have felt more depressed if she'd tried. All she wanted was a hot cup of coffee, a steamy bath and the oblivion of sleep.

Her nerves were tied in a tangle of knots and her stomach felt as if, if she dared to put food in it, it would go into violent revolt. Nothing seemed to bring her peace, not even being back at her beloved house. If she could just remove A.J. from her mind and her heart, she knew she'd feel better, but that would be like trying to siphon off the Atlantic Ocean with a straw.

She sighed and stepped inside the front door, closed it and flipped the dead bolt in place. Leaning back against the door, she sighed deeply, shoved the key into her purse, then made her way down the hall to the kitchen, where she made a pot of coffee, kicked off her shoes and then padded to the living room to wait for it to percolate before taking a bath.

The moonless night shrouded the living room in

deep shadows cut intermittently by the illumination from a streetlight that seeped through the filmy curtains. Picking her way carefully, she made her way to the lamp beside the sofa. She flicked the switch and blinked as the room exploded with light. Straightening, she rubbed at the ache in the small of her back. The aroma of brewing coffee reached her, and she hoped it would be done soon. While she waited, she'd run her bath.

"What took you so long?"

She spun toward the voice and found Kevin Hilary sitting in the chair opposite the sofa, a gun pointed at her chest.

Chapter 14

Sam froze. Kevin in her house pointing a gun at her? Try as she might, she couldn't make it register. The whole scene seemed so ludicrous, so surreal. It had to be a figment of her overtaxed mind or her strained emotions. She blinked, but when she opened her eyes, Kevin was still sitting in her living room with a lethal-looking gun pointed directly at her.

"Kevin? What…what's going on?"

Never taking his gaze from her, Kevin stood and walked forward, his youthful face so serious. "Sloan Whitley. Ever heard of him?"

"Sloan? Of course I've heard of him, but he's dead. He committed suicide. What on earth does he have to do with this?" Though she spoke to Kevin, her gaze never left the gun.

Kevin snickered derisively. "Suicide? It wasn't suicide, Sam. It was murder, and you did it."

Sam's head snapped up. For the first time, her gaze left the gun and centered on Kevin's distraught face. "Me? I had nothing to do with Sloan's death."

Realization hit her like a brick to the side of her head. It was Kevin. Kevin was the one who had been trying to kill her. He was the only one who could have been close enough to her in the hotel fire to activate the tape recorder at just the right time. Kevin had been dancing with her when Joe Santelli told her she'd have to ride home with A.J. Kevin had the opportunity to tamper with her equipment, put something in the food to give the men food poisoning and rig the bomb in her car. And the morning of the attempted fire in her house, Kevin had had brown stains on his hands and clothes, the residue of potassium permanganate.

It was all so simple now. Made perfect sense. Why hadn't she figured it out long ago? Probably because his innocent baby face would make anyone conclude he didn't look old enough to be a fireman, much less a killer.

"Kevin, I did not kill Sloan."

"Ah, but I know you did." A dark cloak of anger slipped over Kevin's features. "*You* lured him into an affair and then *you* walked out on him after *you'd* destroyed his family. *You* made him so despondent about what he'd done that he couldn't face living with the shame. He jumped from his office window because of *you*. *You!*" He shoved the gun under her nose. "And now, *you* are going to pay for it."

His emphasis on *you* caused a cold fear to chase down Sam's spine, but she fixed her features so her expression wouldn't give away her inner terror.

"Kevin," she said, raising her hand as if to ward him off, "I had nothing to do with Sloan Whitley's death. I wasn't even there. I hadn't seen him for months. I broke it off because he was married." She kept her voice soft, controlled, reasonable.

Kevin's expression changed. The hand holding the gun seemed to droop a bit. But he quickly recovered. "You're lying!"

"No, no, I'm not." A fine sheen of sweat broke out on her skin. If she didn't stop him, she was going to die. Her stomach clenched, and her legs wobbled. Sam locked her knees to support herself. Silently, she racked her brain, desperately searching for something that would divert him from his purpose. "I'm—"

The ringing phone cut her explanation off. She glanced down at the caller ID. A.J. Probably making another attempt at explaining his lies. The man never gave up—thank God. This might be her way out. If she could make A.J. understand what was happening and then stall Kevin long enough for A.J. to bring help, she may have a chance.

First she had to get Kevin to let her answer the phone. The phone rang again and again. "I have to get that, Kevin. It's Chief Branson. I'm supposed to meet him, and he knows I'm here. If I don't answer, he'll come here to check on me. You don't want that, do you?" She deliberately kept her tone soft and filled with concern for him.

As if unable to decide, Kevin looked from the phone to her and back again. "Answer it, but be very careful what you say and how you say it. If I think you're pulling something fast, I'll shoot." He shoved the barrel of the gun into her ribs. Pain sliced through her side.

Bile rose up in her throat. She swallowed. Very slowly, she reached for the receiver. Lifting it from the cradle, she placed it to her ear and pressed it tight to prevent A.J.'s end of the conversation from being overheard.

"Hello." She forced her voice to sound normal. Her success surprised her, since her insides had long since turned to quivering jelly.

"Sam, I need to come over. We really need to talk. There's a perfectly good—"

"Hi, honey," Sam said, cutting A.J. off midsentence. "I'm glad you called. Something has come up." She glanced at Kevin. The gun barrel pressed her ribs, reminding her that her life depended on her masquerade. "I'm going to have to cancel our dinner date for tonight."

Dead silence came over the wire. Then he said, "Excuse me?"

Come on, A.J. Don't go stupid on me now.

"Maybe we can make it for tomorrow night. We could go to that little restaurant that overlooks the ocean. The one you like that serves that great shrimp scampi." She knew A.J. had told her about his bad allergy to shellfish, and she hoped he'd remember.

"Hurry it up," Kevin interjected in a whisper, prodding her sore ribs with the gun and shifting nervously from one foot to the other.

Silence again.

"Sam, is something wrong?"

Finally, he'd caught on. "Yes, that's right. Tomorrow night. Okay, see you then." She paused, thinking she may never get the chance to say this again. "A.J.? I love you."

The line went dead. She looked down and saw Kevin's finger on the receiver button.

When she looked up, Kevin was sweating profusely. She'd worked with this kid for months. He was not a killer. Despite the fact that rumor had it his mother got him into the fire academy by sleeping with the fire commissioner, he had a real drive to be a good fireman. If she played her cards right, she might be able to use that to talk him out of this.

"Kevin, you don't really want to do this. You'll be throwing your life away on something you can't do anything about."

"Shut up!"

"Kevin, listen to me. I know you. You're not a killer. You're a fireman and a damned good one. You save lives." His expression grew hesitant, as if her words were getting to him. *Keep talking, Sam.* She hurried on. "You have your whole life ahead of you. You have the opportunity for a wonderful career in the department. If you kill me, the only thing you'll have to look forward to is the death penalty."

His brow furrowed as if he were trying to wrap his mind around what she'd said.

"Kevin."

They both started at the sound of the woman's voice. Sam turned to find Marcia Hilary coming into the room.

Slowly, she walked toward Kevin, her hand extended in front of her.

"Give me the gun, Kevin." Her tone was soft, cajoling.

Kevin's gaze darted between Sam and his mother. His hand began to shake.

Marcia kept walking determinedly toward her son. "The gun, Kevin. Give it to me." The pleading had left her voice and was replaced by the same commanding tone she'd used the night of the ball. "Now."

A whimper escaped Kevin. "No."

Sam held her breath, waiting.

Marcia took another step that brought her to his side. Her hand still extended, she stared into his eyes. "Give…me…the…gun."

As A.J. leaned forward to secure the portable flashing red light to his dashboard, his shoulder holster and gun cut into his side. He winced but focused all his attention on weaving his car through the evening traffic.

Terrible scenarios raced through his mind. He imagined everything from finding Sam dead in a pool of her own blood, to her charred body laying amid the ashes of her home. To save his sanity, he replaced those images with one of what he'd do to the jerk trying to hurt Sam.

Slowly, the chilling dread that had taken command of his senses eased, supplanted by a surging rage at himself for not telling Sam how he felt about her, and at her for not letting him explain, but mostly at the bastard turning her life upside down.

Tires screeching, he careened around a stalled truck and back into his own lane, just as his cell phone rang.

Praying it was Sam telling him she was okay, he flipped it open and pressed it to his ear without checking the caller ID.

"Branson," he barked, his distraught emotions coming through his tone of voice.

"A.J.—" The familiar voice of his best friend came through.

"Luke, Sam's in trouble. I don't know what kind, but there's something going on. I'm on my way there now. Get backup and follow me. No sirens or lights. If someone is in her house and he thinks the cops are coming, there's no telling what he'll do." A brief pause followed. "I want this bastard, Luke."

"So do I. I'm on my way. Don't hang up."

A.J. could hear the sound of Luke scrambling and yelling out orders for backup units to be sent to Sam's address. He followed up the orders with cautions against lights and sirens. Then he could hear the sound of Luke's heavy breathing as he ran across the pavement in the parking lot, followed by the slamming of a car door and the roar of an engine.

"Listen, A.J." Luke fought to control his labored breathing. "The print results are back, and you're not going to believe who's been stalking Sam." He stopped long enough to take a deep breath. "I checked them against the fingerprint file from Engine Company one-oh-eight like you told me to, and it's Kevin Hilary, her rookie partner. His prints are all over the tape recorder."

A.J. slammed his fist against the steering wheel, then guided his car around the corner of Sam's street. "Son of a... Luke, I'm here. I'm parked up the street."

Before Luke could reply, A.J. closed the phone, tossed it on the seat, removed his gun from the shoulder holster and jumped from his car.

As he eased through her neighbors' yards, his thoughts went to what Sam had said before they got cut off. *I love you.* Had that been a part of the act she'd been putting on? Had she meant it? Her tone had sounded very sincere, but A.J. had no way of knowing if she'd forced it to sound that way—or if she were making what she thought was a dying declaration of her feelings for him.

If it had been for the benefit of her captor, the lady was a hell of an actress. If it had been to convince him, A.J. couldn't have asked for better incentive to take this guy down. Just the thought of it being how she truly felt helped melt the frozen ball of apprehension lodged in his chest.

Clearing his mind of everything except finding Sam and making sure nothing happened to her, he pawed his way through a head-high hedge and stepped into her backyard.

At Sam's back window he peered in, but he couldn't see anything. Slowly, staying crouched behind the bushes edging the foundation, he made his way to the front of the house. Through the window, he could see Sam and just the barrel of the gun being pointed at her. A large potted palm blocked the view of the person he now knew to be Kevin Hilary.

A.J.'s heart flipped up into his throat. Thinking Sam may be in mortal danger was one thing. Seeing it damn near killed him.

He glanced over his shoulder for any sign of Luke

and the backup units. Except for his car and the three parked in Sam's driveway, the street was empty. He was on his own.

"Give me the gun, Kevin." Marcia's voice had grown hard, demanding.

Sam could see the hesitation in Kevin's eyes. The fear that had captured Sam's insides turned to stark terror. Tight knots of apprehension formed in her stomach.

Give her the gun, Kevin, Sam pleaded, silently rooting for Marcia.

"Kevin, you know you can't do this," Marcia said.

"I can." Kevin's voice was choked by the tears running down his face.

"You can't. You know that, and so do I. Give the gun to me."

Sam, who had been holding her breath and watching Kevin's finger pressing against the trigger, let out a puff of air and relaxed when she saw his finger slip from the metal loop. Almost in slow motion, Marcia removed the gun from Kevin's limp hand.

"Thank God," Sam said. "For a minute there, I thou—"

Sam's words died on her lips. The barrel was once more pointed at her, but this time, Marcia held the gun, and the evil shining in her eyes told Sam that she'd escaped one death threat only to be faced with another.

"Go outside, Kevin, and get the other things from my car."

"Yes, Mother," Kevin said, and meekly headed for

the door to do her bidding. As he walked, he swiped at the moisture on his face with the sleeve of his shirt.

Marcia stared at Sam, a malevolent gleam in her pale blue eyes.

What did she have planned for her? From the look on the woman's face, it was not going to be pleasant. The terror that had vanished when Marcia took the gun from Kevin returned with a vengeance and settled in Sam's stomach in an icy, cold lump.

A.J. carefully skirted the edge of the porch and eased toward the driveway-side door. As he rounded the corner, he caught his shirt on a particularly lethal-looking rose bush. A long thorn ripped through the material and into the tender skin on the underside of his arm.

"Damn!" he cursed under his breath and jumped clear of the rose bush. Something sharp digging into his spine stopped his backward movement.

"Drop the gun, A.J."

Kevin? But he'd been inside with Sam. If he wasn't in there, then who was holding Sam at gunpoint?

"Drop it!" The pressure on the sharp object lodged against his spine increased as it cut into the skin.

Warm blood trickled down his back. He let the gun fall from his hand. Kevin scooped it from the ground. The pressure of the sharp object disappeared only to be replaced by what A.J. knew to be the barrel of his own weapon.

Chapter 15

Sam tried to ignore the cold threat of the gun pointing at her while she worked at reading what was going through Marcia's twisted mind. "Why are you doing this?"

"Kevin didn't tell you?"

Sam shook her head. What on earth could have compelled the two of them to stalk her and try to kill her? Until Kevin had come to work at the firehouse, Sam had never met either of them. What could they possibly have against her that would push them to these extremes?

But before she could ask, Kevin came back, but not alone. When she saw A.J. walking in front of him with his hands in the air, Sam's heart dropped. A blanket of despondency slipped over her.

Their gazes met, and she saw an apology lingering in the depths of A.J.'s blue eyes. She knew without words that he was regretting that, instead of rescuing her, as he'd obviously planned to do by showing up here, he'd gotten caught and now both of them were trapped. Sam held A.J.'s gaze, trying to silently tell him that she understood.

"Well, well, the big brave police detective has come to rescue his girlfriend." Marcia's sneering tone grated on A.J.'s nerves, but he kept silent. "Get two of the dining room chairs, Kevin. They'll work well for what I have in mind. You two—" using the gun as a pointer, she waved Sam and A.J. to the sofa "—sit."

A.J. pulled Sam down beside him. Sam pressed her thigh against his. Moving his leg slightly, he returned the pressure and hoped that along with it he'd given her a bit of reassurance that they'd find a way out of this mess—together.

"What the hell's going on?" he whispered.

"I don't know. Neither of them will say."

"Shut up!" Marcia glared at them, then looked around her. "Where's the rope?"

"In the car," Kevin said, holding two of the antique wooden chairs Sam had purchased in a little shop on the ocean front. He placed them back to back in the center of the room. "I didn't have time to grab it after I saw him sneaking around."

"Well, go get it now." Marcia's crisp tone lacked any patience. Kevin cringed under her unnecessary attack. "Move," she barked, when he didn't obey her command instantly. "You may not share the same blood, but sometimes you're worse than Sloan."

With their bodies so close, A.J. had no trouble feeling Sam stiffen at the sound of that name. Did she know this Sloan? Though he wanted to ask her, A.J. didn't dare speak and further incur Marcia's wrath.

Kevin left the house, but not until he'd thrown a hateful glare at Marcia. A.J. stored the kid's animosity for his mother away for future reference. Kevin was Marcia's weak link. If he could get him to turn on her, then maybe Sam and he had a chance to get out of here alive. If not...

A.J. tried not to think about that. He desperately wanted a future with Sam and the only way he was going to have one was to keep his head and wait for an opportunity to make his move. But that didn't help to quell the sick feeling lodged in the pit of his gut.

Keeping the gun aimed at them, Marcia backed to the window and did a quick check on Kevin's progress to the car.

Taking advantage of the opportunity, A.J. bent his head. "Who's Sloan?" he whispered to Sam so low, he was sure Marcia hadn't heard.

"A guy I used to date," Sam said, her lips barely moving.

"And how does that connect with this?"

"I don't know."

"I said shut up!" Marcia waved the gun under A.J.'s nose. "One more word out of you and I won't wait to kill your girlfriend."

Sam flinched. She could feel A.J.'s body go rigid.

Marcia must have noticed her reaction. "Those who live with fire, die with fire." Her features twisted into a mask of evil. "Think of this as your...judgment day."

The front door opened, drawing Marcia's attention away from Sam and to her son who had just entered the room carrying a coil of rope and a gas can. Sam's blood ran cold. Marcia's insidious threat found meaning. She was going to burn them up.

Sam could almost smell her own fear oozing from her pores. Vivid reminders of the fire victims she'd seen in the past flashed before her. Bodies curling into fetal positions as a result of the fire's heat sucking moisture from their flesh. Skin so charred it was almost impossible to tell their sex. She shuddered.

"Stop it," A.J. hissed under his breath. Immediately, Sam roused from her morbid memories. "Don't let her get to you. That's what she wants."

"What do you want me to do with this?" Kevin asked, holding up the gas can.

"Put it down. I'll tell you what to do with it when it's time."

Obediently, he did as he was told. "You know, Mother, I could have done this if you'd left me alone," he said, his voice imbued with rebellion.

Sam had never heard Kevin talk to his mother like that. She glanced at A.J., and noted his cunning smile. Instantly, as though their minds were one, she knew what he was thinking. Turn one against the other.

A mocking expression spread over Marcia's face. "I gave you every chance to get rid of her, but you bungled it every time. How long was I supposed to wait?" She made a sound of disgust. "Doesn't surprise me. Sloan couldn't do anything right, either." Anger colored her mumbled words.

Sam waited, listening intently to each scathing word passing between mother and son, while she silently urged Kevin on.

Kevin turned slowly toward his mother, his handsome young face twisted with anger. "Don't you dare talk about my father like that."

Father? Sam came fully alert, all her attention focused on Kevin. Sloan was Kevin's father? Then why didn't they have the same last name? She'd known Sloan was married, but never realized he had a child, too. But that still didn't explain why they were trying to kill her.

"Stepfather," Marcia corrected. "And how do you plan on stopping me? You gonna take me down?" She laughed again. "You couldn't even set a simple fire."

Kevin's shoulders sagged.

Sam gritted her teeth. She hated the way Marcia talked to Kevin, but she hated more that he allowed it. For the first time ever, Sam thought about her sister and the verbal abuse she had taken from their mother. Karen must have felt just like Kevin.

Sam glanced at A.J. His full attention was still on Kevin and his mother.

Don't give up, Kevin, A.J. urged silently. *Keep arguing. Get mad. Get fire-eating mad.*

"Let's face it, Kevin, without me to tell you what to do, you'd go through your whole life falling over your own feet." The young man flinched. Her cruel words seemed to sink into Kevin like a knife being buried in his flesh. "You're weak, just like Sloan was. He didn't have the strength to resist temptation. That's why he got mixed up with this slut." She glared at Sam. "When it came down to the wire, he didn't even have the guts to kill himself."

Blood rushed to A.J.'s temples. "You bitch." Without thinking, he sprang to his feet, his hands clenched into tight fists.

Marcia aimed the gun at Sam's head and glowered at A.J. "Go ahead, Branson. I'd love an excuse to do this right now. I'm not fussy about how or when she dies, only that she does."

Seeing that gun barrel pointed at Sam made A.J.'s insides freeze. Keeping his gaze focused on Marcia, he eased back onto the sofa. Sam grabbed his hand and squeezed. His chest heaved with the effort to control his rage. He'd never felt such intense hatred for another human being in his life. Relaxing his free hand, he willed for his anger to recede. If he didn't get a handle on his rage, he could get them both killed.

"What do you mean my father didn't have the guts to kill himself?" Kevin asked, totally ignoring the heated exchange between Marcia and A.J.

Marcia glanced at her son, then back to A.J. and Sam. "Don't be dense, Kevin. Your stepfather was a weak, mousy man, who couldn't do anything without my help. I helped him run his business, told him what friends to cultivate, made sure he met the right people at the right time and in general pushed him up the ladder of success." She gave a huff of impatience. "If I hadn't helped him over the window ledge, he'd still be standing there thinking about jumping."

Dead silence engulfed the room while they all tried

to absorb Marcia's startling admission. She'd murdered Sloan. A.J.'d already surmised from just listening to her for the past few minutes that Marcia was an irrational, unfeeling bitch, but he hadn't realized how truly evil she was until now.

Feeling her flinch, A.J. squeezed Sam's fingers tighter, warning her to be quiet and let them go at each other's throats.

Kevin broke the silence with an angry whisper. "You killed my father?" He started toward her, his fists at his sides. "You told me Sam was responsible for my father committing suicide. That was why we had to kill her. But he didn't commit suicide, did he? You killed him."

Taking a step backward, Marcia raised the gun level with Kevin's face. "Don't do anything stupid." Kevin stopped his advance. "Now, get the rope and tie these two to the chairs."

A.J. watched Kevin closely. He believed the boy's allegiance was wavering, and three against one was a hell of a lot better than two against two. After all, Marcia had just admitted to killing the one person in Kevin's life that had meant anything to him. But evidently, his allegiance hadn't been shaken quite enough. Kevin shot Marcia a look of pure hatred, but he got the rope, hauled A.J. and Sam to their feet and then pushed them into the back-to-back chairs.

"You don't want to do this, Kevin. Don't let her push you around." Sam's whisper was almost inaudible. "She killed your father. Why would you want to help her?"

"She's right, Kevin," A.J. added. "She'll turn on you

just as fast as she turned on him and on us. You're a witness to her confession. She can't afford to have you around. Who do you think will be next on her list of people to get rid of?" Seeing a gleam of indecision in Kevin's eyes, A.J. allowed a renewed surge of hope to surface inside him. "Don't do it, Kevin. Don't let her ruin your life. Don't—"

"Shut up!" Marcia yelled, evidently having over- heard them. "Hurry up, Kevin."

Glaring at his mother, Kevin wrapped the rope around Sam's wrists, then around A.J.'s. He looped the rope and pulled it tight enough to bite into A.J.'s skin. But then… A.J. felt Kevin slip his finger beneath the rope and loosen the knot.

"It's done," he said, stepping away from them.

As inconspicuously as possible, A.J. tested their bindings. If he folded his palm by laying his thumb along his little finger, he could make his hand small enough to slip free of the rope. He fumbled for Sam's fingers and squeezed. She must have understood and squeezed back.

Marcia came to stand beside them, then grabbed the rope, testing the security of the bindings. Throwing a disgusted look at Kevin, she said, "You can't even do this right. Get the gas can."

When Kevin reached for the can, she tightened the ropes so that A.J. could feel his fingers going numb almost instantly. All hope of them escaping by slipping their bonds drained from him.

"Before you kill us, at least tell us why," Sam said.

Now that Sam and A.J. posed no threat, Marcia sat

on the sofa. As if they were enjoying an evening together, she crossed her long legs and dusted invisible dirt from her white slacks. From her expression and her demeanor, Sam knew Marcia was going to enjoy telling her why she was about to die. If Sam and A.J. hadn't been tied together and Marcia hadn't had a gun pointing at them, Marcia's relaxed attitude would have made it appear as if they were sitting down for a friendly little girl-to-girl talk.

"Why? Well, as for poor Branson," she said, giving A.J. a sympathetic look, "he just happened to stick his nose in where it didn't belong. Lousy timing, Detective." Then she turned to Sam. "But you're going to die because you ruined my family. You stole my husband. After he met you, he didn't want me anymore. That night in his office, he asked me for a divorce so he could marry you. I couldn't let that happen. I'd worked too hard to make Sloan what I wanted. Besides, how would I face my friends?" She stood and strolled casually over to the window. "So, I had to get rid of him."

From the corner of her eye, Sam could see the rage building in Kevin again. She pushed Marcia to dig her hole deeper, to make Kevin angrier.

"But what do I have to do with that? There's no danger from me, anymore." Sam's voice quivered just a fraction. She wanted to add because Marcia didn't have a family anymore, but she thought better of it.

Waving the gun for emphasis, Marcia left the window. "Well, you see, Samantha, I'm a very meticulous woman. I like to have all loose ends tied up. You're a loose end. As long as you're around, I'll be reminded of Sloan's infidelity." Though she was smiling, the humor never reached her cold eyes. "Kevin was supposed to take care of you long ago, but as usual, he bungled the job. I went to a lot of trouble romancing that obnoxious commissioner to get Kevin into the academy and then assigned to your company." Her smile deepened. "And using my last name from my first marriage was a stroke of genius, don't you think? And what did I get for it? I have to finish the job myself because my son is as weak as the man he emulated."

Silence followed as Marcia wallowed in the sheer cleverness of her plan and its outcome.

"Oh, well, enough reminiscing. Time for action. Kevin, pour the gas on those lovely drapes." She indicated the turquoise drapes Sam had had custom-made and had hung proudly at the front window when she'd moved into her house.

But the destruction of the drapes was the least of Sam's worries right now. If they didn't find a way out, more than the drapes would turn to ashes. She tried to gauge the speed with which the fire would spread the several feet to them and how much time they'd have to attempt an escape. It wouldn't be much, and they'd have to move fast if they were to be successful. Once Kevin lit the match and ignited the gas, the wall would turn into an inferno.

Kevin obediently took the gas can and went to the window. Marcia followed but stood close by, better able to oversee his work.

As Kevin doused the drapes liberally with the liquid

accelerant, the pungent smell of gasoline filled the room. Slowly he moved along the wide window, splattering gas liberally on the drapes, wall and floor as he went. Gas hit the wall and ricocheted back, landing on his pants and producing dark spots on the khaki material. Ignoring it, he continued to slosh the gas randomly along the wall.

Absolute, icy terror rolled around in Sam's stomach. She linked her fingers with A.J.'s. Just touching him brought back a tiny bit of the security she'd felt in his arms. If Marcia hadn't been standing so close with the gun trained on them, Sam would have told A.J. all the things that lay hidden in her heart. Instead, she hoped that her touch would transmit some of it to him, and that they'd get out of this mess, and she'd have the opportunity to actually say the words.

She didn't want to die and certainly not this way. No one deserved to die like this. Not her mother. Not her. Not A.J. But right now, she didn't see that they had a way out of it. Overwhelming hopelessness joined the ball of fear.

Marcia moved away. "Make sure you get the wall, too," she instructed.

Following her directions, Kevin splashed gas on the wall. The gas hit and rebounded, and hit Marcia.

"Idiot," she yelled. "Look what you've done." She looked down at the dark patches scattered over her immaculate slacks.

Kevin's movements drew Sam's attention away from Marcia. A ball of stark fear formed inside her as she watched him pull a pack of matches from his pants pocket. He turned toward them and flashed a quick smile. His eyes were moist, and his expression turned sorrowful and apologetic. Then he looked away, lit a match and threw it at his mother.

Chapter 16

Whoosh!

The lit match hit the gas on Marcia's slacks and flames exploded around her like a huge orange flower. She screamed and began running in circles, fanning the flames and making them worse.

"Oh, my God. Kevin, what have you done? Kevin, help me!" Frantically, she beat at the flames, but to no avail. Her screams echoed around the room and blended with the roar of the growling flames.

Kevin smiled and stood his ground. "I don't think so, Mother. I'd just bungle it like I've bungled everything else."

Sam wanted to look away from the horrendous scene taking place before her, but she couldn't.

Marcia's gun fell to the floor with a hollow thud, barely

audible above her screams and the roar of the growing fire. The flames from her slacks caught the drapes and another loud *whoosh* sounded as the entire wall erupted in flames. In seconds, it was a growing inferno. Still, Kevin stood there, his gaze fixed on his mother writhing on the floor, trying in vain to extinguish her burning clothing.

Then she stopped moving. Kevin looked at Sam. The intent in his expression was plain. Sam opened her mouth to try to stop him. Before she could make a sound, he stepped back into the clutches of the orange fingers leaping off the burning drapes. Instantly, he became a pillar of flames.

"Kevin, no!" Sam heard herself screaming, but couldn't stop it. "Kevin!"

Oddly, as if trying to prove to the woman on the floor that he wasn't the worthless coward that she'd labeled him as, he stood silently, never moving a muscle to escape his fate, allowing himself to be burned alive.

Sam turned away. Smoke stung her eyes, but she was certain the tears cascading down her cheeks were not entirely caused by the fire. Forgiveness for Kevin rushed through her mind. In her heart she knew that he would never have done the things he had done without Marcia urging him on, playing on his weakness and dominating him like a drill sergeant. The poor kid hadn't had a chance against a woman with that kind of maniacal evil driving her.

"No time for remorse," A.J. yelled above the roar of the growing fire. "We need to get out of here, or we'll be in the same shape they are."

Sam heard him, but couldn't make her body move. She could do nothing but stare at the spot where Kevin and his mother had died so senselessly. The stink of burned flesh joined that of the burning fabric. Smoke was filling the room.

"Sam!" A.J. nudged her. "Do you hear me? We have to get out of here."

Rousing from her stupor, Sam craned her head to see over her shoulder. "Yes, I hear you, but how do you plan on doing it?" She inhaled a mouthful of smoke. It burned its way down her throat and triggered an intense coughing spasm.

"Your hands are smaller than mine." He stopped to cough. "Can you slip your hand free?"

Sam tried to pull her hand through the loop around her wrist, but it wouldn't move. She strained harder, tearing skin and leaving her flesh raw. Still it wouldn't slip free.

"It's not working."

"Make your hand thinner. Fold your hand…*cough*… lengthwise so your thumb is…*cough*…laying against your little finger and try again." While he talked, A.J. fumbled until he found her hand and then showed her what he meant.

Fear bubbled up inside her. Fear that they wouldn't get out and that they'd die here without ever being able to reconcile their problems and get on with a life together. A fear that should have paralyzed her made her even more determined to get loose. She folded her hand and wiggled it inside the bindings. The rough hemp cut into her flesh. She gritted her teeth against the pain. She could feel her own blood running down her hand. Panic drove her on. She squeezed her hand tighter in the folded position and attempted to work it through the rope loop.

Then it happened. Her thumb's knuckle broke free of the loop, followed by her other fingers. Once the rope dropped from her wrists, it was loose enough for A.J. to free himself, too.

He grabbed her. "Come on," he said, but when they looked up, they were surrounded by flames leaping toward the ceiling. There was no way out.

He covered his mouth with the tail of his shirt. She followed suit and pulled her blouse up to cover her mouth and nose. A.J. dragged her close against his side. "*Cough*…do you trust me?"

She nodded. "Yes."

Outside she could hear the shouts of a lot of men. The fire company had arrived. Her heart gave a leap of hope, but it quickly vanished when reality nosed its way into her thoughts. They were out there, and she and A.J. were trapped in here. If they waited for the firemen to get to them, it would be too late. She and A.J. had no one to rely on but themselves.

The black, acrid smoke had thickened in the few seconds they'd been standing there making a decision. There was no time to think. They had to act—and act fast—if they wanted to live. Fear that had been lingering quietly in her subconscious began creeping into her mind, bringing with it images of her and A.J. dead on the floor beside Marcia and Kevin, their bodies burned beyond recognition. She shook free of her morbid musings, knowing she had no time to be afraid. She looked up at A.J. and gathered strength from him.

"Let's go."

A.J. saw trust in Sam's gaze. It gave him the strength to do what he had to, get them out the only way left to them.

Pulling her close, he leaned down to yell into her ear. "When I say go, run. We're going...*cough*...through that window." He pointed at the window behind a wall of leaping fire. "Keep your shirt over your head... *cough*... Make sure your hair is tucked...*cough*...inside the collar."

Sam nodded, then hoisted her shirt high up her ribs and enveloped her face and hair with it. He did the same.

"Hang on to me." Her arms snaked around his neck and then he felt her lock her fingers together behind his nape. He encircled her with his arms and pulled her face into his chest. "Here we go."

Saying a quick prayer that he wouldn't kill both of them, A.J. closed his eyes and raised his shoulder to absorb most of the impact. Holding Sam as tight as he could, he rushed the window. Momentarily, the heat became unbearable, and he felt it searing the bare flesh on his hands. He bit his lip against the pain, then closed his eyes tighter to block it out.

They hit the window.

Glass shattered.

Cool, clean air rushed at them.

As they plunged forward over the windowsill, A.J. twisted his body to cushion Sam's fall. They hit the ground. Pain ripped through his side. Then he felt cool, damp grass under his hot cheek.

Sam stepped from the ambulance and searched for A.J. in the crowd of people standing around. After Luke and Santelli had scooped them off the lawn and hustled them away from the burning house and into the waiting ambulance to be checked out, things had become a blur for Sam. She knew that at some point Luke had taken A.J. off to talk to him and that Rachel had climbed into the ambulance beside her.

The roaring sound of the crackling fire caught her attention. She turned toward the house, her home. Flames leaped toward the darkened sky. Sparks flew heavenward, kissing the palm fronds on the tree at the corner of the house as they rose and eventually burned out. Three firemen anchored a hose while they directed a heavy stream of silver water on the burning structure.

Sam's heart clenched. Her beloved house had become nothing more than a pile of burning rubble. Tears filled her eyes. She blinked them back. She was getting maudlin about an inanimate object. After all, it wasn't a lost human life. It was just a house, she told herself. Just brick and mortar, wood and paint. Thinking about it in those terms made her feel better.

It *was* just a house. The important thing was who lived in the house. She thought of Rachel and Luke's little family and how warm their home always felt. She'd never felt that same warmth in this house, no matter that the deed was in her name and how hard she worked at making it her own. In all honesty, without the family, her house was no more a home than A.J.'s chrome-and-glass condo.

A.J. Dragging her gaze from the mesmerizing flames, she resumed her search for A.J. Rachel came to stand beside her.

"Do you see A.J. anywhere?"

Rachel scanned the faces in the crowd. "Over there." She pointed toward a small group of men who had just separated, leaving A.J. and Luke standing alone.

Eager to make sure he was okay, she hurried toward him. Rachel followed close behind. As Sam drew close, their conversation reached her ears.

"What about NY?" Luke was gazing at the fire as he asked the question.

A.J. paused for a moment, then said, "There's a lot of loose ends to tie up. In the end, I have to go where my heart leads me."

Sam stopped dead. He was still going to NY. Pain ripped through her.

Rachel came up behind her and put a hand on her shoulder. "What's wrong?"

Sam swiveled and hurried back in the direction from which they'd just come. "Nothing. I...I don't want to bother him now. Can I come home with you?"

"Of course."

"Great. The EMT cleared me to leave. Let's go. I don't want to stay here any longer."

Frowning, Rachel walked beside her as she hurried to the car. Sam climbed in, then slumped in the seat. Rachel got in, started the car and drove off. She glanced at Sam several times as if waiting for her to explain about her rapid departure from the scene, but Sam ignored her.

He was really going. Sam had hoped that after his relentless campaign to explain to her about that damned letter that he'd decided to stay. But she'd been wrong. And then she remembered her impulsive declaration of love. What a fool she'd been. A.J. was a runner. He'd always be a runner. What had ever made her think she could change him?

He'd run from all his relationships. First his wife, then his fiancée. Why would she be any different? Because of a couple of nights of hot sex? If that were so then every man who had ever climbed in bed with a woman would have ended the episode with an on-his-knee proposal.

As they drove past the scene, Sam registered once more that her beloved home lay in ashes. Two body bags lay on the lawn waiting for the forensics people to remove them. She looked away.

Her brain noted the silhouettes of firemen walking through the ruins as they checked for hot spots, but her heart saw only the remains of what was once her front porch, the door that she'd purchased to replace the one with the mail slot, the dark ruins of her custom-made drapes hanging haphazardly from what was left of the broken window frame she and A.J. had dived through. It all seemed like something out of a bad nightmare. Everything she'd built, everything she'd saved for, everything she'd waited for all her life and lovingly assembled around her was gone.

What had she really lost, anyway? A few pieces of

furniture that no children had ever scampered over or bounced on. A front door that had never slammed and announced the arrival of a loved one. A window that had never been smeared with the nose print of a beloved family pet. Gowns that marked a period in her life she would rather forget. A bedroom that would never know the joining of two people in love. All inanimate objects. All replaceable.

Tears threatened, and she blinked them away. The loss of her house was minor compared to the loss of A.J. and a future life with him. A life filled with family and love. The life he'd destroyed by betraying her with lies.

Raging anger welled up in her. Anger at A.J. for all that his lies had stolen from them. Determined not to let Rachel see her emotions, she clenched her hands tightly in her lap. Rachel knew her too well not to notice.

"Sam?" Rachel divided her attention between the road and Sam. "Want to talk about it?"

She shook her head. "No." A moment of ear-splitting silence passed while the pressure to explode swelled inside Sam. Finally, unable to hold back, she spat, "All men are pigs."

Rachel chuckled. "Yeah, but we love 'em anyway."

Sam made no reply.

Her friend paused at a stop sign, then looked pointedly at Sam. "Don't we?"

"Where's Sam?" A.J. was staring at the empty ambulance. The doors were open, but Sam was no longer inside and being tended by the EMTs.

"No idea," Luke said, glancing around them.

A.J. turned toward the sound of a car engine starting in time to see her drive away with Rachel. "Where's she going?"

Luke followed his gaze, then shrugged. "Home with Rach, I guess. We'll catch up with them later. I'm going to need a statement from her anyway."

A.J. looked down at his bandaged wrists and wondered if Sam was just tired and wanted to escape the site of her treasured home lying in smoldering ruins. Or was she trying to escape him?

"So what about the NY job?"

A.J. watched two firemen picking through the fire debris. "I'm going to notify them that I'm turning down the job."

"And the loose ends?"

A moment passed before A.J. replied. "The loose ends are with Sam. We had a bit of a…misunderstanding that needs clearing up."

A heavy sigh issued from Luke. "You didn't screw things up with her, did you?"

Not surprised that Luke had guessed more than a working relationship had developed between him and Sam, A.J. avoided eye contact and nodded. "She found my letter of acceptance to the BCI."

"I'd hardly call that a loose end, my friend. I take it that she didn't know you'd decided not to go."

"She didn't know I was even considering the job. She only found out because I forgot to get rid of the letter. It was on my desk."

"Damn!" Luke ran his fingers through his already

tousled hair. "You're gonna talk to her tonight, right? Get it cleared up?"

A.J. opened his mouth to say yes, but something caught his eye. He stared hard over Luke's shoulder. "Son of a…"

Stepping around Luke, he raced toward a man who was retreating from the scene, the same old man who had been outside the firehouse. The old man Luke had cleared of all the charges. What the hell was he doing here?

"Hey, you!"

The old man stopped and turned toward him. "Are you talking to me?"

"Yeah. What are you doing here?"

For a moment, the old man stared at his feet, then he raised his head and met A.J.'s stern gaze. "I guess you and I better have a talk," he said.

Chapter 17

After the babysitter had gone home, Jay and Maggie were down for the night and the coffeemaker had belched out its last gurgle, Sam and Rachel retired to the kitchen table. The odor of a cinnamon candle burning on the counter filled the air and helped dispel some of the smell of smoke filling Sam's nose.

"So," Rachel said as she poured steaming coffee into a large, orange, earthenware mug that proclaimed It's Good To Be The Queen on its side, "are your ready to talk about why you ran away from the fire scene like a jackrabbit being pursued by a hunter?"

Sam glanced at her friend, then hooked her forefinger in the handle of the mug and twirled it slowly on the slick pine tabletop. "What is there to say?"

Rachel placed the coffeepot on a hot plate she'd positioned between them and then added the sugar bowl and creamer before settling into the seat across from Sam. "Well, there must be something. A woman doesn't declare all men pigs unless something has precipitated that conclusion. Usually it's because something stupid one of those pigs has done has ticked her off somehow—big-time."

"Ticked me off is a fairly benign description of what he's done." Sam glared at Rachel, then rearranged her features. After all, it wasn't Rachel's fault that A.J. was a jerk. "I'm sorry."

"No apology necessary. I've got a tough hide." Laying her hand on Sam's, Rachel grinned. "Hey, if you can't take out your frustrations on a friend, who can you take them out on?"

Sam tried to return the smile, but her face muscles felt as if they were set in a perpetual frown. "He lied to me, Rach."

"About what?"

It was quite telling that Rachel didn't have to ask to whom Sam was referring. After hesitating for a moment, Sam launched into an explanation. "I was in his bedroom…"

Rachel's grin widened. This time it held just a trace of delight.

"Okay, so I went to bed with him. That doesn't erase the fact that he lied to me." Trying her best to hold back angry tears, Sam sipped from her hot coffee. The scalding liquid seared her tongue, and she set the cup down, then glared at her grinning friend. "Dammit! It's not funny, Rach."

Repentance washed over Rachel's expression. She squeezed Sam's fingers. "No, it's not. I'm sorry. Go on."

Obviously Rachel was smiling because Sam and A.J. had gotten together, but she didn't know that, for A.J. at least, it was just a night of fantastic sex. For Sam it had been hope for the future.

"I found a packed suitcase in his closet and asked him where he was going. He told me he'd just come back."

Rachel's brow knitted into a deep frown. "From where? As far as I know A.J. hasn't gone anywhere in the last year, at least nowhere where he'd need a suitcase."

"Bingo!" Sam leaned back in the chair. "Well, I soon found out he wasn't *coming back* from anywhere. He was getting ready to *leave*."

Total unmasked surprise registered on Rachel's face. "Leave for where? Luke didn't say A.J. was going anywhere."

"He's taking a job—" Sam couldn't even say the words without getting choked up. She swallowed hard. "He's taking a job with the New York State BCI."

"What?" Rachel's eyes widened to the size of small saucers. "Why?"

Sam shook her head. "I don't know. Maybe he's running again. Maybe he felt our relationship was getting too close, and he needed to get away before he got caught up in it." She shrugged. "Maybe he just wants to get away from me."

"How do you know all this? Rumor? You know rumors fly around the station house like sparrows migrating south. You can't put any stock in—"

Laying a hand on Rachel's to stop her explanation, Sam sighed. "I found a letter of acceptance in his office."

Rachel slumped back in her chair, obviously at as big a loss as Sam to explain A.J.'s decision or his motives. "You're right. Men are pigs," Rachel whispered.

"I feel like a kid again, Rach. Like my father had just walked out on me. Like…"

All at once, everything—being stalked for weeks, the loss of her house, being held at gunpoint, Kevin and Marcia dying in front of her, A.J. betraying her— seemed to crash down on Sam at one time. Tears began cascading down her cheeks. Silent sobs wracked her body. She buried her face in her hands and let her emotions overflow.

She felt Rachel kneel beside her, then envelop her in her arms. Without saying a word, she held Sam for a long time, until her sobbing turned to hiccups.

"Why don't you go take a shower? I'll leave some of my clothes on the bed for you to change into." Rachel stood and pulled Sam to her feet. "We can talk more after if you want to." Pushing her gently toward the bedroom, she rubbed soothing circles on Sam's back. "Go on. You'll feel better after a nice hot shower."

Though Sam doubted she would ever feel better, she took Rachel's advice and went down the hall to the spare room.

Though her heart still felt as if someone had abraded it with sandpaper and acid, the hot shower had helped Sam relax a bit. She'd towel-dried her hair, rebandaged

the rope abrasions on her wrists with some gauze she'd
found in the medicine cabinet and dressed in the jeans
and blouse Rachel had laid out on the bed. Eager to
have another cup of the coffee waiting for her in the
kitchen, she made her way in that direction. As she
neared the living room doorway, she could hear the
low murmur of voices. Luke must be home.

Dread swamped her. He'd want her statement about
what had happened tonight. The thought of verbally
reliving the last few hours again made Sam feel like a
lead weight had just dropped into her stomach. Pausing
in her forward progress, she almost retraced her steps,
but decided that hiding would just prolong the agony.
She might as well get it over and done with.

Taking a deep breath, she turned the corner and
entered the living room. Luke was behind the bar, an open
bottle of beer in his hand. Rachel stood beside him. Their
heads were close together, their voices barely audible.

"You have to show it to Sam, Luke. She deserves
to see it."

Sam stepped forward. "Show me what?"

Both Rachel and Luke spun toward her, looking for
all the world like they'd been caught with their hands
in the cookie jar. They exchanged hesitant glances, then
Rachel took Sam's arm and led her to the sofa.

"Luke has something you need to see." When Luke
made no move to share whatever it was he had to
show her, Rachel cleared her throat loudly and glared
at him. "Luke."

Reluctantly, Luke bent to retrieve something at his
feet, then came from behind the bar. In his hand was a

brown shopping bag. "I don't know, Rach. I was given this in confidence, and I promised not to reveal what's in here."

Rachel threw him a look that Sam had seen her level on many reporters who had insisted on details of a fire she was not ready to divulge. Sam had dubbed it Rachel's don't-mess-with-me expression. Evidently, Luke was also familiar with the expression. "The bag, Luke."

He brought the bag to the sofa without further argument and took a seat between the two women. Without comment, he reached in the bag an extracted a dog-eared, brown leather scrapbook. Laying it on the coffee table, he opened it to the first yellowed page.

Sam gasped. Glued to the page was a newspaper clipping of her when she'd come in third in the Miss Teenage America Pageant. "Where did you get this?" she asked, turning the page and finding several clippings of her being crowned Miss Florida.

Pain knifed through her heart. It was that night that her mother had died in the motel fire. On the next page were a few clippings reporting the fire and her mother's death.

Luke didn't answer, but she didn't push him. She was too fascinated with the contents of the scrapbook.

The next page held a large clipping of her and her sister Karen arriving in Atlantic City for the Miss America Pageant. She and Karen had argued that night, and Karen had left the next day for New York City and a career as a freelance photographer. Although they'd talked briefly on the phone since then, it was the last time she'd seen her sister face-to-face. Two days later,

Sam decided the pageant circuit had screwed up her life enough, and she pulled out of the pageant and returned to Florida.

For a moment, she had to pull back, look away and take a deep breath to clear her mind. This was giving rise to so many memories she'd kept buried for so long.

"You all right?" Rachel laid her hand on Sam's.

She turned to Luke and tried to smile, but missed the mark by a mile. "Where did you get this?"

"I can't tell you that. I've already betrayed a confidence by just showing it to you." Then he smiled. "I know how much you hated your time in the pageants, but keep going. It gets better, I promise."

Taking him at his word, she turned another page and found her likeness smiling back at her from a news photo of her fire academy graduation. She was in the back row, one of two women, Rachel and herself, and just barely visible above the broad shoulders of one of her fellow graduates. She ran her fingertips over the photo, recalling how elated she'd been that day and how she felt she had finally broken free of her stereotypical childhood image.

The next photo was of her leaving a burning building carrying a child of about five. "That was one of my first fires," she told them.

Then she laughed aloud at the next picture of her receiving a commendation for her act of bravery. When she'd gone back to the firehouse, she'd found her helmet sporting a paper crown and her seat on the truck decorated like a throne.

"Too bad I'm leaving the company." This was a

decision she'd been wrestling with for weeks and tonight she'd finally decided that what she really wanted to do was not run into blazing buildings anymore.

"You're leaving the company? What do you plan on doing?" Rachel asked, her voice holding just a hint of hope.

Sam nodded. "Those times were great, and I'll always remember them and the guys with whom I shared them with love and a smile, but that's not what I want anymore."

Rachel looked deep into Sam's eyes, deep enough that she felt Rachel could see her soul. "What do you want, Sam?"

She met Rachel's gaze. "FIST," she said.

A little squeal of delight escaped from her friend as Rachel leaned past Luke to envelop Sam in a hug. "I'm so glad. I had so hoped you'd make this decision."

"Rach, celebrate later," Luke protested, pushing her off his lap and back to her own side of the sofa. "You started this, so let her finish looking at the book." Now that he'd given it to her, Luke seemed eager to have her see everything.

Sam went back to the book and turning the pages. Each picture showed an important stage in her life: several more fires in which she'd participated, a children's benefit the entire company had attended, a bazaar the company had put on for the children of the community to teach them fire safety and her standing on the stage at the Children's Burn Unit Ball bachelorette auction being bid on like a prize steer.

When she recalled how that night ended in A.J.'s bed, a lump rose in her throat, and she had to swallow several times to dislodge it. No sense crying over something that could never be, she told herself. A.J. was leaving. Period.

But it wasn't until she reached the last page that she paused and had to fight the tears in earnest. The page blurred, and she blinked hard to clear her vision. The photo was worn, as if someone had handled it a lot. It showed a man in his early thirties with a small, black-haired girl wearing a fluffy white dress and a tiny, sparkling tiara sitting on his lap.

"Daddy," she whispered.

So many emotions overcame her at once that she had a difficult time naming them: sadness, anger, longing, regret and then overpowering love. With the tip of her finger, she traced her father's beloved face. If she closed her eyes, she could feel the roughness of his beard against her skin, smell his aftershave, and hear his laughter.

How odd that she would have such a strong emotional reaction to a man who'd deserted her and Karen. She should hate him, and she did in some ways, but, as she looked at the photo, the overwhelming feeling she experienced was love. Although she rarely admitted it even to herself, considering the kind of life he had led with her mother, it was no wonder he'd opted to just leave.

However, that didn't make her heart ache less. It didn't fill in all those years without him. Most of all, it didn't forgive him for leaving her with a woman who wanted her only for the glory and prize money Sam could bring her. Although she loved him, Sam wasn't sure she could ever forgive him.

She closed the album and pushed it away from her. "Where did this come from?" she finally asked Luke.

"Your father assembled it. He's kept track of you for the last few years and every time you appeared in the newspapers, he'd cut out the article and add it to the scrapbook."

Steeling herself against the rush of love she felt when she realized that her dad had been hovering in the background of her life, Sam stared at Luke. In her heart, she hoped he would say, *Your father gave it to me.*

"No, I mean how did you come to have it?"

"Remember the old man from the firehouse?" She nodded. "He gave it to me. He said he knew your dad. He said he'd want you to have it."

The old man? Sam's heart dropped to somewhere below the floor of the living room. "But I thought he was a suspect."

"He was until I talked to him and cleared him."

She wondered if this man had been a friend of her father's, someone she could find and talk to about the man who had helped create her. "Who is he? Where can I find him?"

Luke hesitated for a moment. "His name's Ted. I'm sure you can find him in the park across from the firehouse. He gave me the scrapbook the day after we questioned him."

Luke took a sip from his beer and avoided Sam's gaze.

"I can't believe you knew this and kept it from me."

With her frustrated need to know more and her anger at Luke for not sharing this sooner beating at her, she couldn't control the torrent of questions racing through her mind. "Did A.J. know about this? Where's my father? Did the old man tell you?"

He sighed. "No. A.J. didn't know." He leaned forward and rested his elbows on his knees. "Sam, he didn't say where your dad is. I'm not sure he knows."

She stood. "I have to go."

"Where?" Rachel asked, standing, too.

"To find Ted and see if he knows where my father is."

Just before Sam closed the front door behind her, she heard Rachel say, "Stop her."

To which Luke replied, "No, she needs to do this, Rach."

Sam wandered blindly through the darkened trees. Their shadows fell across the gravel park path, their black fingers slipping over her like ghosts as she walked. Streetlights illuminated the vacant park benches she passed, but she didn't notice them or where she was walking. Instead, she scanned the darkness for a lone figure, a familiar figure that had been a phantom in her life for the past few weeks—the man who had given Luke the scrapbook and might know where to find her father.

Why she thought she'd find the old man here at this time of night was a mystery to her. She just knew she had to try.

She'd been concentrating so hard on finding the old man that she hadn't given one thought to the carelessness of her impetuous actions. Wandering around in a public park after dark was not the smartest thing she'd ever done. But by the time that registered with her, she heard the sound of footsteps following her.

Chapter 18

Sam began walking faster, cursing her stupidity for coming here at this time of night. She'd done some pretty stupid things in her life, but endangering her safety had not been one of them—until now.

The footsteps grew closer.

Cold sweat broke out on her forehead and not because she was overheated, despite her race to outrun the footsteps. Fear gathered in the pit of her stomach, fear akin to what she'd felt when tied to A.J. in her living room while they waited for an insane woman to either shoot them or burn them alive.

Speeding up her retreat, Sam hurried past several palm trees lining the path. The footsteps behind her sped up. She stumbled and almost fell, but strong hands caught her just in time.

Struggling to free herself, she spun toward her captor. Even if the shadowed figure hadn't been as familiar to her as her own mirrored reflection, she would have known him simply by the hollow feeling that had invaded her stomach and the rapid pulsing of her heart in her temples at his touch.

"What are you doing here?"

A.J. looked down at her. "Don't worry. I'm not here to make you listen to me. I got the message. You aren't interested." His voice was flat, resigned.

Sam wanted badly to just wrap her arms around him and tell him everything would be all right if he'd just stay. But she didn't. That had to be his decision and, obviously, he was not opting to stay. "Then why are you following me?" She looked pointedly at his hand, where it still rested on her shoulder.

A.J. released her and stepped back. "Luke called and told me where you'd be. He and Rachel were worried that something would happen to you."

"Well," she said, raising her arms out to either side of her so he could see she was unharmed. Fighting off the need to fall into the circle of his arms and take refuge from the events of the evening, she stepped away. "As you can see, I'm fine. You can go now."

Deliberately, she kept her voice cold and emotionless while she worked to tamp down the unreasonable pain arising from the fact that he'd given up so easily on them. But she supposed she could expect no less. She'd been running from him ever since the fire. Truth be known, she was afraid if she stopped running and he caught her, she'd open herself up to more of his lies and more pain.

A.J. made no move to walk away, nor did he touch her again. "I'm not leaving until I introduce you to someone who wants to speak to you." He stepped to the side. "Luke told me you were looking for him, so I picked him up and brought him here."

For the first time, Sam noticed the silhouette of another man standing in the shadows behind A.J., but she couldn't see his face. When the man moved forward and the streetlight hit his still-semishadowed features, she recognized the old man from the firehouse.

"Are you Ted?"

What she could make out of his expression was tinged with sadness. "Hello, Sammi Girl."

The name resonated through Sam like the blast from a shotgun. Her heart contracted. Pain arrowed through her. Only one person had ever called her that. But this man looked nothing like him. The father she remembered was tall, straight, young and full of life. This hunched-over man looked as if he carried the troubles of the world on his bent shoulders. His weathered, lined face showed years of hard living flavored with many trials and tribulations.

"Who are you?" she finally asked, unable to allow herself to believe her own eyes. "How do you know my father? How do you know his nickname for me?"

The old man stepped into the glow of a streetlamp. His face finally was fully illuminated. He smiled. "I know that name because I gave it to you the day they laid you in my arms in the hospital. From that time on you were always my Sammi Girl."

More than the words, now that she could see his

whole face, Sam recognized the light twinkling in his eyes. That devil-may-care look that always appeared when she'd done something her mother was outraged by, but that he thought was funny and perfectly acceptable for a little girl with a big imagination.

Awash in a storm of emotions she couldn't control, Sam looked around frantically for A.J. She needed him, his support, his strength. But he'd vanished. Only she and this man remained in the darkened park.

Sam fought to concentrate on anything but what was happening. The sound of a night bird singing from somewhere beyond the circle of the streetlamp's halo of light. Waves beating hypnotically against the shore beyond the perimeter of park grass. The roar of an occasional car passing on the street. Her own heart pounding beneath her blouse.

When she could no longer shut out him or his identity, her wobbly knees gave out, and she plopped onto the nearest bench. With tears blurring her vision, she raised her face to the man standing silently before her.

"Daddy?"

He nodded. "Yes, Sammi."

"But Luke said—"

"Don't blame him. He didn't know. I told him I was a friend of your father's." He squatted down in front of her, making sure they didn't touch. "He never made any other connection because our last names are different. Mine's Warren and yours is Ellis, your mother's maiden name. You always knew me as Nathan Theodore Warren. I only recently started answering to Ted."

A tangle of emotions assaulted her. She wanted to scream to the heavens that her father was back. At the same time she wanted to hit him for all the lonely nights she'd spent since she was ten years old, for leaving without saying goodbye, for never coming back. All of it came rushing down on her, pounding away at her nerves until they broke through her emotional barriers.

Unheeded tears cascaded down Sam's cheeks and choked off her throat. She swallowed repeatedly to clear them. "Why?" The question that had haunted her for almost twenty years fell from her lips on a sob. "Why did you leave us?"

Her father straightened, sighed, then took a seat next to her on the bench. "It's not a very pretty story, Sammi. Are you sure you want to hear it?"

Tears choking off her words, she nodded. She'd waited years for this explanation, and she wasn't about to give up the chance to finally get an answer.

"Do you remember when your momma started entering you in those beauty pageants?"

"Yes. I think I was five." Turning sideways on the bench, she linked her hand around her ankle and drew her leg under her while she silently drank in the sight of him.

"You had just turned five. When she first talked about entering you in those damned pageants, I should have said no." He spread his hands in a helpless gesture. "I thought she'd do it a few times, then get tired of it. But after she'd entered you in five or six pageants and you won them all, it seemed she only got more addicted to it." He shook his head and ran his hand over his face, then raised his gaze to the darkened ocean beyond. "I tried to stop her. Told her both you girls needed a normal childhood and a permanent home with a dog and friends, but she wouldn't listen.

"I was traveling back and forth to my job at the time. It was the only way I could have time with my family. One night we had a terrible fight about it. I left in a huff to catch a plane back home so I could go to work the next day. When I came back a week later, you were all gone."

"Why didn't you come after us?"

He glanced at Sam. "I tried. I asked the motel owner and the pageant people about where you'd gone, figuring she'd have left an address for me to catch up with you, but she didn't. None of them could tell me. I called everywhere I could think of and asked if Samantha Warren was entered in their pageant. But no one of that name was there."

Sam straightened. She recalled a time when her mother decided Sam should be entered under her mother's maiden name of Ellis. She'd given Sam some half-baked excuse about it being better to prevent any weird pageant groupies from finding her.

"We all started going under her maiden name for anything to do with the pageants. Momma said, because I was in the public eye so much, I was at risk of being attacked, and it would make it harder for pedophiles and child molesters to find me." She recalled that she hadn't even been sure what pedophiles and molesters were back then. And her mother never explained. All she knew was that they were bad people and that after that she'd been terrified of stepping on a stage.

He laughed without humor. "It took me almost six years, but I finally found that out."

My God! All these years she'd blamed her father, and it had always been her mother's fault. She bowed her head. "I am so sorry. All this time—"

"No." A warm hand covered hers for a moment. "It's not your fault, Sammi." He sighed. "Maybe I just didn't work hard enough to convince your mother to go home. Maybe I didn't look hard enough."

A large yellow Lab slipped out of the shadows, lumbered over to Sam and smelled her hand. After finding nothing of interest and allowing Sam to scratch him behind the ear for a moment, he raced off in response to a whistle from the man walking down the beach a few hundred yards away from them.

"You should have had one of them, Sammi Girl. Every kid should have a dog."

"Motels don't allow pets," she said, hearing not her voice, but her mother saying the words in her head. "Dad?" The word fell from her lips so naturally.

He turned to her, his mouth breaking into a huge smile that tugged at Sam's memory. For ten years, that smile had been the last thing she'd seen every night before she closed her eyes. Then suddenly, one day it had been gone. Pain pierced her heart. Pain as fresh as the day when her father had gone out of her young life.

"Once you knew about the name thing, why didn't you try to find us?"

"I did, but it had been so long I figured your momma had told you tales that would have poisoned you against me, and that by then you and Karen hated me. So, once

I did find you all, I stayed in the background. I took early retirement so I could travel around the pageant circuit and keep an eye on both you and Karen. Then when you left the circuit, I arranged to spend summers in NY where Karen is and winters here near you."

"That's how you got the photos and newspaper clippings?"

He nodded. "I was…no, I *am* so proud of you." His voice choked with emotion. For a long moment, he looked at her as if he couldn't get enough of the sight of her. Then he swallowed hard. "Sammi, I know it's been a long time and a lot has happened, but… Do you think that we could… That maybe… Oh, hell." He looked away and ran his hand through his thinning salt-and-pepper hair.

Sam's heart swelled inside her. She laid a hand on his. "Yes, I think we could."

With a muffled sob, her dad enveloped her in his arms. Sam felt like that little girl in the tiara again, the little girl that would cuddle on her daddy's lap and feel comforted and protected against the world.

"I love you, Dad," she said against his shoulder.

"I love you, too, Sammi Girl, always have, always will."

"You won't go away again, will you?"

"Not on your life," he said and squeezed her close. "Not on your life."

He sat straight and held her at arm's length. "Don't you think it's time that you talked to that young man who brought me here? I may be wrong but I think he loves you a lot. Otherwise, why would he have threatened me within an inch of my life not to hurt you?" Her father motioned to the deep shadows not far from where they sat. "And why is he standing guard over you over there?"

Sam turned her gaze in that direction. Leaning against a palm tree and buried in the shadows was the silhouette of a man—A.J.

Chapter 19

"Hi, Sam." A.J. straightened at Sam's approach. His voice sounded strained.

Sam stared at him for a long time, then checked back to see if her father was still there, but the bench was as empty as the park, except for the two of them.

"Why are you still here? I thought you had given up trying to make me listen."

A.J. stared at her. "I'm not sure I'll ever really give up on you, Sam."

She studied him, trying to judge his sincerity. But his face remained blank, so she pivoted on her heel and prepared to leave.

"Sam, please. You can't keep avoiding me."

"I can try," she mumbled. But her retreat had come

to a halt. She waited, contrarily hoping he'd come after her, stop her.

"Yes, you can run, but what is it going to accomplish? Won't you please talk about this?"

Anger spiked through her. Anger that had been building since the day she saw the packed suitcase. She spun to face him. "Talk about what? That you've been planning to leave all along? That you lied to me about the suitcase?" Suddenly she didn't want to hear his lies, his feeble explanations, his excuses. When he opened his mouth to speak, she shook her head. "Never mind, A.J. You don't owe me any explanations. After all, there's nothing between us except a couple of nights of great sex."

She turned away again, but was stopped by two strong hands settling on her shoulders, hands that sent shivers down her body. She bit her lip and tried to fight off the waves of longing and the urge to throw herself into his arms, to accept any explanation he gave her just as long as they were together.

A.J. curled his fingers into the material of her blouse to keep her from leaving. "You may be able to convince anyone else that all we had was sex. You also may be able to convince yourself. But I was there, Sam. I was an active participant. It was a hell of a lot more than two people getting physical satisfaction."

He was right. For her it had been a commitment. For her it had been a beginning. But what had it been for A.J.? She turned to ask him, but decided that she couldn't stand it if he said nothing or, even worse, if he lied and said it meant a lot. With her battered emotions about at the end of their rope, she knew she'd give in to A.J.'s pleas.

A.J. waited, but she remained silent. Neither did she make any attempt to extract herself from his hold on her. He took heart from that.

Exerting a little extra pressure, he turned her to face him. "Please. Let's talk."

Against her better judgment he was sure, Sam allowed him to lead her back to the park bench. He pressed her down and then sat beside her, hoping she wouldn't make a dash for her car. If he inhaled deeply, he could smell the flowery-scented shampoo wafting from her. He wanted to touch her, to hold her. But he was afraid he'd spook her.

Instead, he just looked at her, taking in her shiny hair, her scrubbed look, her presence. What he didn't want to see was her face. He hated himself for the look of betrayal in her tear-reddened eyes.

"You and your dad okay?"

She nodded.

"Good."

"Small talk, A.J.? Is that why you wanted me to stay here, to make idle conversation?" She made a move to stand.

"No, that's not why I asked you to stay."

She took a deep shuddering breath. "Why, then?" she said, her voice shaky. Blinking, she looked away and cleared her throat. "Why did you lie to me? Why did you let me believe you cared?"

"Because I do." He held his breath, waiting for her reaction.

Her head snapped around. She stared into his eyes, as if gauging his sincerity. He made himself hold her gaze, afraid that the slightest flicker on his part would make her doubt the truth of what he'd said.

"You do?" she finally said, her voice barely above a whisper. "Then why did you lie to me about that suitcase? Why were you leaving?"

A.J. started to answer, but stopped. Gentle raindrops spattered his face and the ground around them. Slowly, the rain increased. Lightning split the sky and thunder rolled ominously across the darkened heavens.

"Come back to my house with me?" She frowned. He held up his hands. "I promise. Just to talk. Nothing else."

For a moment, he thought she was going to refuse, but then she nodded. "Okay."

They ran through the rain to his car. Once there she sent her own car, parked at least a block away, a covetous glance.

"You'll get drenched. Just get in my car."

She hesitated, then climbed in. A.J. slipped behind the steering wheel, started the engine, and pulled into the late evening traffic before she could change her mind.

As A.J.'s car cruised through the night and the strained silence between them went unbroken, Sam wondered why she'd said okay to going to his condo. What could he possibly say or do that would make things right between them?

Her preoccupation with what lay ahead disappeared when A.J. pulled the car into his condo parking slot.

Instead, unease took over her thoughts. Was it wise to intentionally put herself in such an intimate setting with him? Her heart sped up, and blood pumped through her temples.

"Can't we talk here?" she asked when he opened his door to get out.

A.J. paused, leaned back in the seat without closing his door, sighed deeply, then turned to her. "Sam, I promised this would be just talking. Do you trust me so little that you'd think I'd break my word?"

Had he ever broken his word to her? Had he ever not done something he'd promised to do? She couldn't recall one such instance. Still, she studied him before agreeing to go inside. The light burning beside his front door illuminated his face, leaving deep shadows where it didn't touch. His mouth was set in a straight line. His eyes bore into hers.

Did she trust him to keep his word? Just as that question flitted through her mind, he smiled and the fight drained out of her.

"Okay. Let's go inside." God, when it came to A.J., she was so easy it sickened her.

Inside the condo, she was again struck by the lack of A.J. in the place. The AC kicked in and blew chilled air onto her from a vent above her head. The icy air and the coldness of her surroundings seemed to seep into her rain-dampened clothes, and she wrapped her arms around her middle in an effort to dispel the feeling.

A.J. disappeared down the hall that led to his bedroom. When he returned, he was carrying two thick white bath towels. He gave her one and then rubbed the water from his dripping hair with the other.

"Can I get you something?" A.J. asked, obviously putting off the moment of truth. "Coffee? A mixed drink?"

The thought of a stiff mixed drink was nice, but she needed her head clear for what was to come. Warm coffee, on the other hand, was very appealing. "Coffee, please."

He nodded then disappeared into the kitchen. She could hear the sound of him making a pot of coffee, followed by the sounds of him assembling cups and spoons on a tray. When the noise stopped, she expected him to return to the living room while the coffee brewed, but he remained in the kitchen.

Rehearsing his story? she wondered.

While she waited, the uneasy tension gathering in the pit of her stomach increased. This was a mistake. She never should have come here with him. What if he came back in here and told her he was still leaving? What if she broke down and made an ass of herself? Clenching her hands together in her lap, she gave herself a stern lecture.

You are not going to make a fool of yourself, because you are not going to let him know how much you care. You've been able to mask your feelings all your life. This is no time to let them run amok. Besides, he said he cared for you. Maybe he's not going anywhere.

She stopped that vein of thought abruptly. Building up her hopes was one certain way of slashing her heart to ribbons when that hope sank as quickly as the Titanic. She vowed not to expect the worst, but also not to expect anything else, either. Neutral was her best defense against heartache with A. J. Branson.

A.J. called himself every kind of coward for not going back into the living room while the coffee brewed. But he couldn't. He couldn't stand sitting next to Sam and acting as if he felt nothing for her, as if he'd never held her in his arms.

He loved the woman, and he had no idea how to prove it, to regain her trust. While he listened to the muffled gurgle of the coffeepot, he leaned against the kitchen counter and wracked his brain for a way out of the mess he'd made for himself.

If he'd just destroyed that damned letter. But it wasn't just the letter. She'd found the suitcase. What had ever possessed him to pack the suitcase before he'd been ready to leave?

Lord, but she was a stubborn woman. He let a smile creep across his face. He'd had to all but hog-tie her to keep her off that fire truck when her life was on the line. But that was one of the things he liked most about her. She was courageous, and didn't run from life.

When the coffeepot emitted its last gurgle, he sighed, retrieved the pot and set it on the tray with the mugs and the rest of the coffee makings. This wasn't going to be easy but, when it came to the rest of his life, he could be just as stubborn as Miss Samantha Ellis.

By the time A.J. carried the coffee tray into the living room, Sam had fortified herself to accept whatever came along.

Picking up the earthenware mug he'd set before her, she curled her fingers around it and absorbed the heat radiating from it. The warmth transferred to her damp skin and removed some of the chill she'd experienced upon entering the condo. Rather than looking at the man sitting silently beside her, she stared down into the steaming, fragrant, dark liquid and tried to still the urge to put down the mug and run.

But running from her problems was not something Sam did. Unlike A.J., who hit the road at the first sign of emotional trouble, she had learned to take a stand, fight it and defeat it.

Or bury it so deep you never have to face it, a little voice chimed in.

Finally, A.J. set his cup down and swung around to face her. "The letter you found was my acceptance of a job with the BCI in New York."

"That much was pretty clear," she said, also setting her cup down. "What I don't understand is why you couldn't be honest with me about it when I asked you about the suitcase."

He looked away, then back to her. "I don't know why I lied about the suitcase. When you found it, I had all intentions of accepting that job and making tracks out of Florida. Maybe I just didn't want to have to explain why I was leaving."

"And now?"

"Now, I've realized that everything I want is right here."

There had been no pause before he answered her. No hesitation in his voice. Still, Sam was terrified to believe him. When all she'd ever wanted was the truth, so many people had lied to her. So many of the people she'd trusted with her happiness had betrayed her. How did she know A.J. wasn't one of them?

"So, does that mean you're not going to take the job?"

"Yes. I'm staying."

Again, her skeptical nature kicked in. A.J. must have read the doubt in her expression because before she could protest, he had grabbed her hand and pulled her into the bedroom with him. Once there, he seated her on the end of the bed, then pulled the suitcase from the closet. One by one he removed the clothes and stashed them in their respective storage places. When he'd finished putting his clothes away, he zipped the suitcase and stowed it on the top shelf of the closet.

He turned to face her. "Now do you believe me?" When she didn't answer immediately, A.J. came to her and knelt in front of her. "Sam, I've only ever said this to two women before, and they eventually walked out of my life. One because she couldn't stand the idea of being married to a man who faced possible death on a daily basis, the other because, for one reason or another, she decided that being married to another cop wouldn't allow her to do *her* job well. So saying this now is a huge risk for me, and one I swore I'd never take again. Then I met you." He paused and took her hand, then looked deep into her eyes. "I love you, Sam, and as long as there's a chance you love me and that we can make a future together, I'm sticking as close to you as I can."

He released her and then stood. "I know the word around the station house is that I ran from those women, but I didn't. They ran from my job. But *was* I running? You bet I was. I was running from love. I wasn't about to put my heart on the chopping block again…until now."

Though A.J.'s words should have removed all of Sam's misgivings, they didn't. Instead, they invoked a whole new array of questions. Could she take a chance on him? Could she lay her heart on the line again?

To find her answer, she looked deep into his eyes. There, she saw sincerity, devotion and affirmation of his declaration of love.

"Is there a chance, Sam? Do you love me? I know you said it on the phone, but I wasn't sure if that was your heart talking or a woman who was playing a game with a man who had a gun at her head." He ran a finger down her cheek. "There's no gun to your head now. Do you love me?"

With his words, Sam's heart swelled so much, she was sure if she looked down it would be pushing through her chest. Suddenly memories flashed through her mind. Memories of his caring protection of her, of his gentleness after she'd almost died in a car crash and a fire. Memories of his gentle but passionate lovemaking. Memories that he'd been the first person in her life to see beyond her surface and find the real Samantha Ellis, the one who cared about people, who was… What were the words he'd used? Intelligent, compassionate, fiercely loyal, brave and…loving?

If she hadn't been blinded by her anger, she would have seen long ago that those were not the words or actions of someone who didn't care deeply. They came from a man who cherished a woman beyond all else. The kind of man she'd dreamed of all her life. It was time she stopped talking herself out of what she wanted and what she felt.

She touched his face. "When Kevin had the gun to my head, my heart was speaking to you. I would have said it even if my life hadn't been in the balance. I was afraid I'd never get the chance to tell you. So, just to clear up any doubts you may have, I do love you. With all my heart."

The words passed Sam's lips on such a soft whisper, if there had been one noise in the room besides their breathing, A.J. wouldn't have heard them. He started to reach for her, but stopped himself. He'd promised they'd just talk, and he was not about to start down this new path of their relationship by breaking his promise. But, God, how he wanted to.

The bed behind them was so inviting, so tempting. This wasn't about just sex. It was about the rest of their lives. He closed his eyes against the need and struggled with his control. Once he had it harnessed, he opened his eyes again.

Sam held his gaze with hers. Slowly, she ran her tongue over her lips, leaving them moist and inviting. He took a deep breath and his insides flipped. Under this kind of sexual pressure, he wasn't sure how long he could hold on to his good intentions.

Continuing to hold his gaze, she stood, took one step toward him, stared into his eyes, then walked her fingers up his chest. "I know you said only talk, but I'm really tired of talking," she murmured against his lips. "How about you?"

He smiled slyly and whispered, "As my dear old granny always said, actions speak louder than words." He lowered his head and engulfed her mouth with his.

Heat and sensations far beyond his ability to put words to crashed over him. He held Sam close, infinitely grateful that he'd been given this opportunity, one he never thought would be his again.

The kiss was passionate but tender and so much more. It was love in its deepest, purest form. It was a silent promise between them that they would have a life together. They would have a family, build a house—

A.J. suddenly remembered that Sam had lost her treasured possession, her house, the place she had bought, decorated and loved.

Catching his breath, he leaned away from her and stroked the side of her face with the back of his hand. "I'm sorry about your home. I know how much it meant to you. I know—"

She laid a finger over his lips, then nuzzled her face into his chest and tightened her arms around him. "Thank you for caring, but it was never a home. I didn't realize that until I saw the smoldering ruins. As long as no family ever warmed its rooms and filled them with love and laughter, it would have never been a home. Rachel and Luke have a home. What I had was a house."

He kissed the top of her head. "We'll build another one, sweetheart. One we can share. One we can fill with screaming kids. One with a porch where, when we grow old, we can while away the hours in our rocking chairs together while our grandchildren play on the lawn." He leaned away to see into her face and grinned. "What do you say, Sam?"

The pictures he'd drawn swirled through Sam's mind, bringing with them a warmth and security she'd never known before. A. J. Branson was the best thing that had ever happened to her. And to think she'd almost driven him away.

Sam laughed and kissed him quickly. "Was that a proposal, Detective Branson?"

"It certainly was, Miss Ellis."

"Miss Warren," she corrected.

He kissed her again. "Miss Warren."

He took a deep breath and held her at arm's length. "I know there will be bumps in the road to come. I also know I'll spend more than one hour holding my breath outside a blazing building waiting for you to reappear, and I know that life with you is going to be a roller-coaster ride, but I don't care because life without you would be hell."

Standing on tiptoe, she kissed him soundly. "What do you think about me leaving the fire company and concentrating on working full-time with Rachel in FIST?"

Trying not to be obvious, A.J. breathed a sigh of relief. "That's got to be your decision, Sam. I won't lie and say I wouldn't be happier if I never had to stand outside a blazing building waiting for you to emerge unhurt, but I won't try to make your decision for you."

"In the last few weeks, I've almost burned up in my own home, nearly got blown up in my car, almost died in a car crash and a fire." She ticked them off on her fingers, then stopped. "No, make that almost died in *two* fires." Her forehead knitted in a thoughtful frown. "If I were a cat, I'd have four more lives to play with. Since I'm not, I think I'd better quit while I'm ahead and concentrate on putting out the fires we start right here." She nodded toward his big king-size bed.

A.J. hugged her close. "Then I'll just have to work overtime keeping you happy as a member of FIST and just Mrs. Branson. So what do you say? Marry me?"

"In that case, my answer is yes!" She threw her arms around his neck and hung on while he whirled her around the room, both of them laughing like kids.

He stopped, let her slide down his front and then captured her lips in a deep kiss full of promise and love and a fistful of forevers.

Sam pulled back just a bit and looked deep into A.J.'s eyes. "For the record, there is nothing *just* about Mrs. A. J. Branson. It will be one of the most important roles I've ever played." Then she frowned. "I always have meant to ask you. What does the A.J. stand for?"

He laughed. "Austin Jedadiah."

Sam laughed and kissed him. "A.J. will do just fine."

"So will Sam," he murmured, steering her toward the big bed, and knowing that as long as Sam was in his life, he would always be touched by fire in one way or another.

Epilogue

A white-and-yellow birthday cake sat in the middle of a table laden with gifts. Sam's father had ordered it for A.J., so the writing said Happy Birthday, Sammi Girl. Every time she read it, she experienced a surge of warmth for the two men who had made it a point to throw her her very first birthday party, complete with cake, hats, noisemakers and a clown.

It had been almost a year since she'd met her father in the park and every day had been a joy of rediscovery for them. Best of all, he'd been there to give her away six months ago when she'd promised to spend her life with A.J. in a ceremony with all the trimmings, just as she'd always dreamed her wedding would be. The only thing missing had been Karen.

Though she'd sent her an invitation, Karen had sent

a reply that she'd had a photo shoot scheduled for that day and couldn't make it, but maybe she'd see her soon. Sam had told A.J. that she doubted that would happen, but she would not give up the hope that one day, her family would be reunited.

The next day, a package containing a silver cake knife, engraved with Sam's and A.J.'s names and their wedding date, arrived from Karen. The card accompanying the package simply said Always, Karen.

"Hey, this is no time for a frown," her dad said from behind her. "I want you to open my present."

"I was going to open all my gifts later, Dad."

He laughed. "I think you'd better open this one now."

He led her to the center of the room where a large box sat in the middle of the living room floor. Every once in a while the box shivered. She glanced at her father, but he just shrugged and grinned.

Sam got on her knees beside the box and reached for the enormous red bow on the top. The box not only shivered, but this time it made a muffled noise. Again she looked to her dad for an explanation. He had plastered a noncommittal expression on his face.

"You gonna open it or look at it?" he said.

Tentatively, she removed the bow and then the paper. The cardboard box began to shiver more vigorously. Sam pulled up a flap and a golden ball of fur jumped into her lap. She caught it and lifted it up to look at. It was a golden retriever puppy with a big pink bow around her neck.

"I told you every kid needs a dog," her father whispered close to her ear.

She smiled up at him, kissed his cheek and whispered, "Thank you." The dog licked both their faces and they laughed. The sound of her father's laughter filled Sam with untold warmth.

"I'd take her for walk if I were you," her dad said. "She's been cooped up in that box for a bit."

"She?" A.J. said from behind them. "Just what I need. Another female to order me around."

"Lily," she declared. "Her name is Lily." Laughing, Sam stood, tucked Lily under her arm and kissed A.J. soundly on the mouth. "And as for being ordered around…you know you love it."

For a moment, he looked skeptical, then he grinned. "Yeah. I do." And he did. Not that Sam did all that much ordering. She'd been so consumed with decorating their first house and getting reacquainted with her father that she hadn't had time to do much of anything else.

Just then, the doorbell sounded. A.J. took Lily from Sam and handed her to Rachel. "Can you take our furry child out for a quick walk?"

"Sure. Come on, you darling thing." As she walked toward the back door, Maggie and Jay, who was just starting to walk, joined her.

"You come with us," he told Ted. A.J. steered Sam toward the door. "If I'm right, this is your other present from me."

Sam was shocked. He'd already given her a magnificent diamond tennis bracelet, an oil painting of their wedding photo and a party that would live in her memory forever. What more could there be?

He positioned Sam in front of him, then swung open

the door. Both Sam and Ted gasped. Standing on the front porch, partially hidden by a large package wrapped in blue-and-yellow birthday paper, was Karen.

"Happy birthday, little sister."

Sam couldn't speak. She hadn't seen Karen in years. Tears ran down her cheeks. She opened her arms and Karen stepped into them. Another pair of arms encircled them both from behind.

"My girls," her father murmured, and Sam felt the moisture from his tears on her face.

A.J. stood a few feet away and watched Sam, her sister and her father. Every time Sam smiled, every time she laughed, he was reminded of how much she'd missed over the years. His heart still ached for the child who had missed out on her childhood. But she'd found her family, and now that A.J. would always be around to watch over her, he'd see to it that she never missed out on anything ever again, and that she knew nothing but days filled with love and laughter.

* * * * *

Silhouette® Romantic Suspense
keeps getting hotter!
Turn the page for a sneak preview
of Wendy Rosnau's latest SPY GAMES *title*
SLEEPING WITH DANGER

Available November 2007

Silhouette® Romantic Suspense—
Sparked by Danger, Fueled by Passion!

Melita had been expecting a chaste quick kiss of the generic variety. But this kiss with Sully was the kind that sparked a dying flame to life. The kind of kiss you can't plan for. The kind of kiss memories are built on.

The memory of her murdered lover, Nemo, came to her then and she made a starved little noise in the back of her throat. She raised her arms and threaded her fingers through Sully's hair, pulled him closer. Felt his body settle, then melt into her.

In that instant her hunger for him grew, and his for her. She pressed herself to him with more urgency, and he responded in kind.

Melita came out of her kiss-induced memory of Nemo with a start. "Wait a minute." She pushed Sully away from her. "You bastard!"

She spit two nasty words at him in Greek, then wiped his kiss from her lips.

"I thought you deserved some solid proof that I'm still in one piece." He started for the door. "The clock's ticking, honey. Come on, let's get out of here."

"That's it? You sucker me into kissing you, and that's all you have to say?"

"I'm sorry. How's that?"

He didn't sound sorry in the least. "You're—"

"Getting out of this godforsaken prison cell. Stop whining and let's go."

"Not if I was being shot at sunrise. Go. You deserve whatever you get if you walk out that door."

He turned back. "Freedom is what I'm going to get."

"A second of freedom before the guards in the hall shoot you." She jammed her hands on her hips. "And to think I was worried about you."

"If you're staying behind, it's no skin off my ass."

"Wait! What about our deal?"

"You just said you're not coming. Make up your mind."

"Have you forgotten we need a boat?"

"How could I? You keep harping on it."

"I'm not going without a boat. And those guards out there aren't going to just let you walk out of here. You need me and we need a plan."

"I already have a plan. I'm getting out of here. That's the plan."

"I should have realized that you never intended to take me with you from the very beginning. You're a liar and a coward."

Of everything she had read, there was nothing in

Sully Paxton's file that hinted he was a coward, but it was the one word that seemed to register in that one-track mind of his. The look he nailed her with a second later was pure venom.

He came at her so quickly she didn't have time to get out of his way. "You know I'm not a coward."

"Prove it. Give me until dawn. I need one more night to put everything in place before we leave the island."

"You're asking me to stay in this cell one more night...and trust you?"

"Yes."

He snorted. "Yesterday you knew they were planning to harm me, but instead of doing something about it you went to bed and never gave me a second thought. Suppose tonight you do the same. By tomorrow I might damn well be in my grave."

"Okay, I screwed up. I won't do it again." Melita sucked in a ragged breath. "I can't leave this minute. Dawn, Sully. Wait until dawn." When he looked as if he was about to say no, she pleaded, "Please wait for me."

"You're asking a lot. The door's open now. I would be a fool to hang around here and trust that you'll be back."

"What you can trust is that I want off this island as badly as you do, and you're my only hope."

"I must be crazy."

"Is that a yes?"

"Dammit!" He turned his back on her. Swore twice more.

"You won't be sorry."

He turned around. "I already am. How about we seal this new deal?"

He was staring at her lips. Suddenly Melita knew what he expected. "We already sealed it."

"One more. You enjoyed it. Admit it."

"I enjoyed it because I was kissing someone else."

He laughed. "That's a good one."

"It's true. It might have been your lips, but it wasn't you I was kissing."

"If that's your excuse for wanting to kiss me, then—"

"I was kissing Nemo."

"What's a nemo?"

Melita gave Sully a look that clearly told him that he was trespassing on sacred ground. She was about to enforce it with a warning when a voice in the hall jerked them both to attention.

She bolted away from the wall. "Get back in bed. Hurry. I'll be here before dawn."

She didn't reach the door before he snagged her arm, pulled her up against him and planted a kiss on her lips that took her completely by surprise.

When he released her, he said, "If you're confused about who just kissed you, the name's Sully. I'll be here waiting at dawn. Don't be late."

Romantic
SUSPENSE

**Sparked by Danger,
Fueled by Passion.**

Onyxx agent Sully Paxton's only chance of
survival lies in the hands of his enemy's daughter
Melita Krizova. He doesn't know he's a pawn in the
beautiful island girl's own plan for escape. Can
they survive their ruses and their fiery attraction?

*Look for the next installment in the
Spy Games miniseries,*

Sleeping with Danger

by Wendy Rosnau

Available November 2007 wherever you buy books.

At forty, Maureen Hart suddenly finds herself juggling men. Man #1: her six-year-old grandson, left with her while his mother goes off to compete for a million dollars on reality TV. Maureen is delighted, but to Man #2—her fiancé—the little boy represents an intrusion on their time. Then Man #3, the boy's paternal grandfather, offers to take the child off her hands…
and maybe even sweep Maureen off her feet….

Look for
I'M YOUR MAN
by
SUSAN CROSBY

Available November wherever you buy books.

For a sneak peek, visit
TheNextNovel.com

ATHENA FORCE
Heart-pounding romance and thrilling adventure.

History repeats itself...unless she can stop it.

Investigative reporter Winter Archer is thrown into writing a biography of Athena Academy's founder. But someone out there will stop at nothing—not even murder—to ensure that long-buried secrets remain hidden.

ATHENA FORCE

Will the women of Athena unravel Arachne's powerful web of blackmail and death...or succumb to their enemies' deadly secrets?

Look for

VENDETTA
by *Meredith Fletcher*

*Available November
wherever you buy books.*

REQUEST YOUR FREE BOOKS!

2 FREE NOVELS PLUS 2 FREE GIFTS!

Silhouette® Romantic

SUSPENSE

Sparked by Danger, Fueled by Passion!

YES! Please send me 2 FREE Silhouette® Romantic Suspense novels and my 2 FREE gifts. After receiving them, if I don't wish to receive any more books, I can return the shipping statement marked "cancel." If I don't cancel, I will receive 4 brand-new novels every month and be billed just $4.24 per book in the U.S., or $4.99 per book in Canada, plus 25¢ shipping and handling per book plus applicable taxes, if any*. That's a savings of at least 15% off the cover price! I understand that accepting the 2 free books and gifts places me under no obligation to buy anything. I can always return a shipment and cancel at any time. Even if I never buy another book from Silhouette, the two free books and gifts are mine to keep forever.

240 SDN EEX6   340 SDN EEYJ

Name	(PLEASE PRINT)

Address	Apt. #

City	State/Prov.	Zip/Postal Code

Signature (if under 18, a parent or guardian must sign)

Mail to the Silhouette Reader Service™:
IN U.S.A.: P.O. Box 1867, Buffalo, NY 14240-1867
IN CANADA: P.O. Box 609, Fort Erie, Ontario L2A 5X3

Not valid to current Silhouette Intimate Moments subscribers.

Want to try two free books from another line?
Call 1-800-873-8635 or visit www.morefreebooks.com.

* Terms and prices subject to change without notice. NY residents add applicable sales tax. Canadian residents will be charged applicable provincial taxes and GST. This offer is limited to one order per household. All orders subject to approval. Credit or debit balances in a customer's account(s) may be offset by any other outstanding balance owed by or to the customer. Please allow 4 to 6 weeks for delivery.

Your Privacy: Silhouette is committed to protecting your privacy. Our Privacy Policy is available online at www.eHarlequin.com or upon request from the Reader Service. From time to time we make our lists of customers available to reputable firms who may have a product or service of interest to you. If you would prefer we not share your name and address, please check here. ☐

SRS07

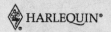

HARLEQUIN®

Mediterranean NIGHTS™

*Not everything is above board
on Alexandra's Dream!*

*Enjoy plenty of secrets, drama and sensuality
in the latest from Mediterranean Nights.*

Coming in November 2007...

BELOW DECK

by

Dorien Kelly

Determined to protect her young son,
widow Mei Lin Wang keeps him hidden
aboard *Alexandra's Dream* under cover of
her job. But life gets extremely complicated
when the ship's security officer, Gideon Dayan,
is piqued by the mystery surrounding this
beautiful, haunted woman....

HARLEQUIN *Romance*

New York Times bestselling author

DIANA PALMER

Handsome, eligible ranch owner Stuart York knew Ivy Conley was too young for him, so he closed his heart to her and sent her away—despite the fireworks between them. Now, years later, Ivy is determined not to be treated like a little girl anymore…but for some reason, Stuart is always fighting her battles for her. And safe in Stuart's arms makes Ivy feel like a woman…his woman.

Winter Roses

Available November.

Silhouette®
Romantic
SUSPENSE

COMING NEXT MONTH

#1487 HOLIDAY HEROES—"The Best Noel" by Rachel Lee, "Christmas at His Command" by Catherine Mann
Jump into the holiday season with two military-themed short stories by *New York Times* bestselling author Rachel Lee and RITA® Award-winning author Catherine Mann.

#1488 KISS OR KILL—Lyn Stone
Mission: Impassioned
When undercover agent Renee Leblanc recognizes Lazlo operative Mark Alexander at a secret meeting, she fears her alias will be blown. Mark realizes Renee is following the same lead and proposes they partner up...but their passion for one another could be deadly.

#1489 SLEEPING WITH DANGER—Wendy Rosnau
Spy Games
Onyxx agent Sully Paxton's only chance of survival lies in the hands of his enemy's daughter, Melita Krizova. He doesn't know he's a pawn in the beautiful island girl's own plan for escape. Can they survive each other's ruses and their fiery attraction?

#1490 SEDUCING THE MERCENARY—Loreth Anne White
Shadow Soldiers
To the rest of the world, Jean-Charles Laroque is a dangerous tyrant. But Dr. Emily Carlin gains access to his true identity and in doing so becomes a captive in his game of deception and betrayal—all the while falling under the mercenary's seductive spell.

SRSCNM1007